THIS BOOK
BETRAYS
MY BROTHER

KAGISO LESEGO MOLOPE

MAWENZI
HOUSE

We acknowledge the support of the Canada Council for the Arts for our publishing program. We also acknowledge support from the Government of Ontario through the Ontario Arts Council.

ONTARIO ARTS COUNCIL
CONSEIL DES ARTS DE L'ONTARIO
an Ontario government agency
un organisme du gouvernement de l'Ontario

Canada Council   Conseil des arts
for the Arts   du Canada

Cover design by JD&J Design LLC

Library and Archives Canada Cataloguing in Publication

Molope, Kagiso Lesego, 1976-, author
     This book betrays my brother / Kagiso Lesego Molope.

Originally published: Cape Town : Oxford University Press Southern
     Africa, July 2012.

Issued in print and electronic formats.
ISBN 978-1-988449-29-6 (softcover).--ISBN 978-1-988449-30-2 (HTML)

     I. Title.

PS8576.O45165T55 2018   C813'.6   C2018-901435-0
                                                C2018-901436-9

Printed and bound in Canada by Coach House Printing

Mawenzi House Publishers Ltd.
39 Woburn Avenue (B)
Toronto, Ontario M5M 1K5
Canada
www.mawenzihouse.com

For my Sisters
Choarelo, Tumelo, and Lopang

And in honour of Kwezi, for her bravery

Attitudes toward other creatures [are] conditioned by one's level of security within the universe.

Dr Mamphela Ramphele

A man ain't nothing but a man. But a son?
Well now, that's *somebody*.

Toni Morrison, *Beloved*

PROLOGUE

TO UNDERSTAND MY BROTHER'S importance, they say you have to picture a wedding ceremony. Not the one they call a White Wedding, where the bride wears white and only those who are invited attend. No. I mean the big one, the traditional wedding, the one where everyone and their second cousin comes, invited or not. They say you must picture the dancing, the singing, the drinking, the cooking, and the dust rising and falling beneath the many dancing feet as they go up and down the street singing and ululating and inviting neighbours to join them.

Imagine all this, they say, but at the centre of it all, place a baby. A little baby boy.

I am told that the news of my brother's birth spread to the south, to the east, and so far north that it crossed the border and went into Botswana, where it was welcomed joyously by aging and long-lost relatives. My parents received letters and telephone calls from places neither of them had ever even visited. This was not simply a birth, but a great and momentous family event.

A son, in my mother's family, had been in people's wishes and prayers for many years. In fact, if you look back on the family tree you will see that all the males there are spouses, not children born to a long line of matriarchs. You will see that the last time there was a baby boy, he was my great-great-great-grandmother's brother, and he died in infancy.

The thing about family history is that it all depends on the person you speak to. There may be agreements here and there, but the story you walk away with depends on what the person telling it wishes to reveal and, perhaps more importantly, not to reveal. I tend to file away what I am told in my head with a little note saying who told me the story. I think they should be labelled like the gospels, as in: The Gospel According to Paul or The Gospel According to Peter. I say: The Day I Started Walking, According to Papa; The Day Basi Won the Maths Prize, According to Mama; or What People Thought When Mama Was Expecting Basi, According to Mama. It helps me make sense of a lot of things.

This is all a bit tricky when you are a child, of course. But you learn, as I have learned, to pick and choose your storytellers very, very carefully.

Case in point: a distant, often-drunk aunt whom I only ever met a handful of times, revealed to me that there were boys outside the family fathered by some of the men on the family tree. Children unacknowledged. But she is, like I said, a distant relative. And a drunk. I couldn't tell you how we are related except that it's through my father's side—and this is a large part of what discredits her.

In any case, you could listen to rumours about unacknowledged babies, but of course you'd be a fool because what you hear outside the family is not true. Let's call them *ditori*, a popular way of saying "lies" where I'm from.

What matters are family stories as told by the women who lived them. What they say is closest to the truth.

What is not disputed is that my great-great-grandmother had three sisters and four daughters, my great-grandmother had two daughters, and her own two sisters only bore girls. Our mother was our grandmother's third and final girl child.

My mother has told me in my aunts' absence that there were times when her sisters knew—just *knew*, in that way that only women can—that they were carrying boys. They could feel it. It was from the way the baby kicked, or from how high the baby was lying in the womb, how high they were carrying. "The nose can tell you," I've heard women say. "If a woman's nose is wider and larger when she's pregnant, then she's having a boy. You're prettier when carrying a girl." Or: "Look at how sick she is at the beginning. Only a boy makes you this sick."

My aunts, according to Mama, would walk down the street and some elderly woman would call out, "It's a boy! Just look at that nose!" In my mother's case, as we know, they were mistaken. *She* knew when she was carrying a boy. She never needed any of the old women to tell her what was going on inside her. "He was so fierce," she would say with an easy laugh, her eyes going up to the ceiling as if her whole body was transported back to that time, as if she were pregnant again.

"He kicked when there was noise. He kicked harder when people clapped—always the star. Eish!" she'd say, holding her belly with both hands. "I never slept with him in here. Never slept. As if the waiting was too long for him."

The point is, she *knew*. It was difficult for her sisters, she understood. So many years and so many hopes dashed. That was heartbreaking, she could see, but when it was her turn, well . . . it was her turn.

After all those decades, after the praying and the hoping and the medicine—"Oh! The medicine!" my mother would exclaim, rolling her eyes to let us know that hers was pure luck and had nothing to do with medicine—the gods finally delivered my brother, Basimane. OK, let me say, it was not just luck. To my mother it was like she was *chosen* to bear a son. "I always knew it would end with me," she still says. "When I was growing up I always thought this thing, this curse or whatever you want to call it, was not going to affect me." She laughs heartily, with much satisfaction, when she adds, "I was right."

"Here was that first glimmer of light in a dark cell," was what my aunt Tumo, who has been a political prisoner a few times, liked to say about Basi's birth. It's not until now, actually, that I note the heavy sarcasm in that sentence.

"This one was strong," they all told us, a veiled reference to the other one, the one who died mere months after his birth. The one whose name I don't believe I ever heard because who dares to name a curse? Who would beckon a bad omen?

No, Basimane was made of everything strong and beautiful and promising.

So you can say, then, that I am nothing special. This I know—not like a thorn constantly digging into my little toe, but more the way you understand that the wind is colder in the winter and warmer in the summer. It just is that way.

"You don't understand, Naledi," my mother used to say to me. "It was the happiest day of my life. The happiest day of all of our lives," she'd add, her left hand sweeping across the room and the gold rings on her fingers catching the light.

All of our lives.

It has been understood by both strangers and friends that Basi—as we affectionately call my brother—is as special as raindrops on dying crops. I say this not with jealousy but with apology, really; an honest, heartfelt, and heartbreaking apology coming from a sister's guilt. It is my way of explaining him and what he did—lest you judge him too harshly after you listen to what I am about to tell you. Or maybe it is my way of apologizing just because I *am* about to tell you this, my side of the story. What my mother would call my *ditori*.

Family history is called that because it is told *by* the family, *for* the family. When you recall your relatives' lives, you are supposed to create beautiful poetry. What you do is turn the light on them and adjust it just so, accentuating their features. You choose the best colours, you paint a halo and then you watch them glow. Perhaps by the end of this book you'll ask: What's wrong with you then, telling it like this? Using dim lighting and all the wrong colours?

My mother asks the same thing.

My brother, by the way, would never tell, would never have told, if the tables were turned. Telling would not even have been an option for him. He would have taken it to his grave. Ask anyone who has ever known him. Ask his friends, his teachers, everyone. They will all tell you that Basimane—or as his friends lovingly call him, Bafana—is a pillar of loyalty, a rock.

But, like I said, I am nothing special.

I should say that all of this is coming up now because . . . you see, I saw Moipone last week. In town, at a Wimpy. Not that I haven't thought of her, of course. Not that I haven't spent many nights waking up sweating or lonely days vomiting when the memory of those few weeks comes back to harass me.

I saw her and I thought, what else? She looked gorgeous. I wondered . . . well, I wondered a lot of things. Was she well? What had happened later? I mean, of course, not only weeks after the last time I'd seen her, but years later. Had there been, for her, even a day when she had not thought about it? Probably not a day, but an hour or two? Does she ever look back and think, gratefully, that she has just passed a whole hour without thinking about it? I've had those moments when I find myself laughing and joking and then I laugh and joke some more because I've just realized that, *tjerr*! I haven't thought about it for a little bit, have I? I'm so thankful in those times, for those minutes that pass without it all haunting me.

I didn't know if I had the right to ask. What *is* the thing to say to Moipone? What do I have the right to ask? And then there's this . . . *connection*, this allegiance I've always felt with her. Well, it's quite inappropriate, isn't it? I don't know. I think that it may be. My strongest allegiance should be to family, as my mother and all my family have reminded me many times.

When I saw Moipone, well, the whole thing was very quick and I felt rather uneasy and awkward. My hands and feet felt foreign to me. I fidgeted a bit. The expression on my face was even harder to control. I noticed that her scar is still there and she noticed that I was looking at it, the small mark—which must have been black at first but is now a shiny colour only slightly darker than her skin—that sits on her chin in a curve. A neatly carved birthmark is what you'd think it was if you didn't know the story. It even looks pretty, if I forget for a moment how it got there. It all got a lot more awkward then, because I was terribly embarrassed that she had seen me staring at the scar.

Then there's the thing she said, which wasn't entirely inappropriate, but rather cruel and all the more shocking coming from her. I mean her, as in the way I *remember* her. She's a lot older now. She's probably not at all the same, given what happened.

Ugh! Of course, me being the way I am and my dreams working the way they do, I've hardly slept well since.

1

MARAPONG, MEANING "THE PLACE OF THE BONES" or "where the bones are"—note the subtle difference—is where I come from. "What came first?" people like to ask about the name. Were the bones there first or were the people there first? I still have no idea. I know our people were moved here from somewhere else, a place now occupied by White people.

Marapong is not the sort of place you stumble upon. To get to it, you have to follow the instructions—if you remember them. Stay on the road and turn at the right places. One arrives there only after fully experiencing that unnerving feeling of being lost in a strange country with a strange language. You begin to come undone, just a little bit. Re-read directions—the major maps are not specific—wonder if perhaps you may have missed a sign while your thoughts wavered. Maybe you think: *I should have had my full attention on this, turned off the radio, not reached for another handful of chips.* It is as if the plan is to make you think you've made some sort of miscalculation. But just as you say your prayers, wipe a damp forehead or shift uncomfortably in your warm seat, then what do you know: you're there!

I remember often feeling great relief at the sight of the first houses leading into the place, even having grown up there. Here I'll let you in on a little-known fact: there's just one sign that actually says "Marapong," followed by an arrow and giving no estimation of the distance. You'll see signs for Rustenburg, which is quite far from Marapong, actually, though Marapong is on the way. Aha! You see? The secret is: the fewer the number of kilometres on the Rustenburg signs, the closer you are to Marapong. I don't know if it helps for me to add that Rustenburg is actually four hundred kilometres from Marapong, but there you are.

You see? Knowing a little more about the place: that's the trick. I know the road from Pretoria to Marapong like I know the inside of my own home because every day we would drive about forty minutes to and from school.

If you arrive in the early evening you'll see smoke billowing from chimneys in the distance, marking the end of another day; to your left and right, on the dusty ground, women with children packing up the fruit they have been selling all day at the side of the road. You know a good day by the amount of produce going back into the bakkie. The less fruit and vegetables you see, the better. Then there are the many, many clusters of small houses painted in dazzling colours—the brightest brights—and small windows and chimneys protruding from the rooftops. Taxis whizz by, overtaking each other, anxious to get just one last run before the customers are all home for the night, braking and stopping without warning. You might catch the tail end of a Teddy Pendergrass song as you're being overtaken by a posh taxi (the sixteen-seater), or it may be Mariah Carey. Or maybe the taxi going by is an old grungy Toyota that seats twenty-four—then, more likely, you might hear gospel.

What you will not hear from your car is the passenger in the taxi ahead of you yelling, "*Mo phasiching!*" or, "*Mo khoneng!*" You'll just see the abrupt stop, taxi veering off the road in front of you, dust rising, people scattering.

So, after that nerve-racking drive into Kasi, don't settle in: be ready for anything. Keep your eyes open and your foot on the brake.

Buses go at the same speed as the smallest car, and they also go along narrow dusty roads, sending the person on a bicycle fleeing for safety. Best not be behind a bus, then. As you get closer you'll see children playing just one last game of *khati*, mothers taking the day's washing off the line.

If you've arrived in the morning you will see this same scene in reverse: bakkies unloading, the women hawkers laying down blankets for their children and themselves to sit on all day. Up go the large garden umbrellas, down comes the fruit. Passengers are getting into instead of jumping out of the taxis, but the taxis are always, always in a rush in all directions. The smoke from the chimneys is there, but there's less than what you would see in the evening—a lot of people save their coal and kindling for the family's evening meal. The women are sweeping the yard instead of taking down the washing (hanging it up comes in a bit later in the day) and the children, instead of playing, are in uniform with shiny, Vaseline-smothered legs, hair perfectly brushed. They are carrying large school bags and walking to school.

But come at high noon and you must shield your eyes: from a distance you don't see the cluster of houses as much as you see the roofs. You'll understand why people have named this area Silver City. The sun, at its fiercest hour, beats off the iron roofs, creating a glittering sea of silver.

In the lower end of Kasi you'll note the bakkie surrounded by people awaiting their weekly supply of water. They carry very large buckets and enormous containers, and they wait for the young man with water to serve them for a price. His face is serious, determined. This is the face of someone who knows the cost of losing his job. The silver sea has no running water, no indoor toilets, only outhouses, no trees, only rocks and dust. This is the lowest part, before the slope rises.

In all locations—and I think even in the suburbs—wealth follows the lay of the land. The higher you go up the hill, the larger, grander and farther apart the houses are, and the closer you get to cars, running water, and indoor toilets. The boundaries get more pronounced: from wire fences to brick walls, and then the walls get higher and higher and you may start to think you've come full circle, that you've just driven back into town.

This is the place of my birth, the stage for all the scenes of my childhood.

2

WHEN I WAS GROWING UP, Marapong was like most townships, or as we called it: the location, *loc'shin, lekeishene,* or *Kasi.* Then, as now, the end of the school year spells sheer euphoria for everyone. December is like an intoxicating storm, one that we welcome as if we've spent the rest of the year looking up and saying rain prayers, waiting for the sky to wail. Have you heard the songs that come out of locations? First of all, any album worth listening to is released in December, and the songs often mention the time of the year. In northern countries songs are about summertime, but here you will hear "December." One of the more popular songs the year before I left home for varsity starts with: "Hello! Hello, December!"

The end of the school year brings longer days, and summer hailstorms that are followed by a gorgeous blazing sun. It brings the chance to reinvent yourself, become someone new at the beginning of the following year. Then there is the seduction of large, ripe peaches; sweet-smelling apricots in all their orange-yellowish glory; sweet mango madness; and, of course, lush grapes hanging down from sturdy vines in people's yards, providing shade and perfect green or purple bunches.

Girls kick off their shoes and tuck their skirts or dresses into the elastic of their panties, playing *khati, legusha,* and any other game you can play without leaving the street. Boys, on the other hand, are allowed to go. They kick off their shoes, roll up their pants and run away. They move through Kasi in groups, like lion packs hunting. What they do together stays secret for the most part—unless, like me you're lucky enough to have a brother who trusts you and lets one or two secrets slip.

Marapong is on unusually fertile land for a location. This kind of land is rare because the point of most *loc'shins* was to build them where nothing much can grow. In those days the hill was like a jungle, with overgrown and surprisingly lush ground that turned green in summer and yellow in winter. We used to call that part *nageng* or "the woods," although I should say that a more fitting translation would be "the wild."

Before we moved up the hill to the Extension—"*diEx*"—the boys used to go swimming, and my brother brought details of the woods to me. He told me there were trees and overgrown weeds, strange fruit you're not supposed to eat; and snakes. And there was also mysterious life there: a woman's handbag, a pair of men's pants. You would find love letters underneath some shrubs and a blood-stained sheet at the base of a tall tree. Things happened there that most of us couldn't explain. I fed the details to my friends who didn't have brothers who ran in the wild, and in turn we would weave elaborate tales of what happened up there.

When we were younger, before we moved, in the woods where the ground begins its sudden rise away from Kasi, just after the second main road, there was a large and rather deep hole in the ground. What you see there now are houses—mansions on the hill and the first double-storeys many of us had ever seen. But there used to be that hole. Just beyond the high bushes.

Well, the hole had been there for years, untouched except for the times when the rainstorms came and filled it with water so that it appeared—to the boys—to be a large, muddy swimming pool, which they called "the chocolate pool." That was where they went to cool off during the arresting December heat. They would run like wild horses up the hill, tear off their clothes and hang them up neatly on the tree branches—because they were all township boys raised by mothers who taught them to fold their clothes and hang them up nicely—and dive into the pool. It was then that Basi learned to swim—and I would later remember this every time he won a medal for his skills in an Olympic-sized swimming pool.

On these excursions, the boys told each other stories and jokes. They discussed the mysterious objects they saw in the woods and came to all sorts of conclusions. In fact, the first time I heard about sex was when my brother came back and told me that they had been walking up through a particularly heavily wooded area when they heard what he called "a woman's cries." I had at first been startled and asked if she had been hurt, but Basi smiled and said they were "happy cries." The boys had warned each other to be quiet and had crouched behind a tree, and that was when they had seen a man and a woman. Naked.

"You'll know these things as you get older," Basi told me. He must have been twelve years old then, which means that I must have been eight. When I told my friends, we decided that there could be no such thing as "happy cries" when a woman was naked with a man. None of us would have liked it if a boy saw us naked, would we?

By the time my family had moved up the hill, my brother was older and there was no chocolate pool, only a big white house in its place. He still had fond memories of his long afternoons spent swimming with the boys from Kasi—much to my mother's chagrin, because she wished Basi would stop having anything to do with the old boys.

"They're not classy," she would say, frowning at my brother, pursing her lips and angrily waving her arm in the air, her gold bangles like wind chimes in a storm. "We didn't move up here and send you to the best school so you could keep walking around with . . . them!" She would throw her hand towards the window as if discarding some undesirable object outside.

Basi wouldn't say anything, which I think made my mother feel desperate. Then she would repeat it and add, "Don't you see *gore a le tshwane na?*"

Those were some of my mother's favourite words: "We are not the same." At these times she sounded like the noise of a passing ambulance. It was loud and hurt your ears, but you knew it would soon pass.

It was really all for nothing; I knew Basi would never let those boys go. It was like asking him to cut a limb off his own body.

"They're my brothers," he'd tell me when we were alone, hitting his chest with a fervour he'd never adopt in my mother's presence. "They know me better than anyone will ever know me. *Anyone!*" he'd say with furious eyes glaring in the direction of the house, or looking into my eyes, as if daring me to refute his declaration.

It terrified my mother that he continued to cross the gulf between our old life and our new life. That he did it so carelessly made it that much more puzzling to her. She would suggest new friends, guys who went to the same schools as we did—private schools in town—whose families had moved up the hill or out to the suburbs. Often, after school, she would park our large red Mercedes in the parking area at the front of the school yard, and chat with Moabi's mother or Themba's father, exchanging stories about the joys and perils of owning a business ("Oh, I love that I can just leave anytime," "Ah, helpers are so tiresome!") or talking about our schools and the next rugby match. She would come back to us and gleefully say things like, "Moabi's father would like it if we stayed at the same hotel when we go to Durban for the holidays. *Akere* you and Moabi can spend time together? Do what you boys like to do. Let's see what your father says, *nè*?"

Basi would nod distractedly, then once he was home he would quickly be out of his uniform, into his jeans and running down the hill to see Kgosi, a boy he had been best friends with since they were small children in primary school.

Now, Kgosi may as well have been my brother's twin. In laying down the facts as neatly as memory allows, I must state that they were unrelated and only friends. If you knew them, you would assume they were brothers and it would never occur to them to correct you—they were so close that calling them friends seems inadequate. They wore each other's clothes (to my mother's horror). They had similar facial expressions and a language that only the two of them understood. They used words that were strange to the rest of us, signals, handshakes, whistle calls (some of them practically songs, they were so long and elaborate) and they would turn the collars of their shirts up or down to tell each other something.

No surprise then that Basi and Kgosi were together when they saw the woman's body.

3

IT WAS A SCORCHING December afternoon, six months after our move up to *di*Ex. Basi was still in that phase where he was pretending (for our mother's benefit, and only she believed him) not to be spending much time with Kgosi any more. He was like an undercover detective, watching our mother's every move, asking her questions about where she was going and when she would be back so that he could time her departure with Kgosi's arrival. He would phone Mabatho, a girl who lived two houses away from Kgosi, because Kgosi's family didn't have a phone; she would hang up the phone, run out to Kgosi's house and bring him back to her house. My brother would phone a few minutes later (impeccably timed, he liked to brag), when Kgosi would pick up the phone. They would arrange when to meet and Kgosi would come up as soon as my mother had gone out. As always, Basi was diligent to a point where I could imagine him in the future working successfully as a spy.

But something happened that day that made my mother change her mind, and she turned back after Kgosi had already started walking up the hill.

Along with four other boys, Kgosi arrived too soon, and saw our mother's car still parked outside. I was upstairs in my room, and I watched them duck behind a neighbour's van as my mother took her time in the driveway. I was squinting against the morning sun that flooded through the window of my room, wanting to see who the other four boys were—but they all had their backs to our house as they hid behind the truck. All I could see were their neatly shaven heads and newly broadening shoulders, their clean clothes ironed and crisp.

To my left, in front of the garage, my mother slung her handbag over her shoulder and clicked her heels together as if to get rid of dirt—even though there probably was none, this was a long-standing habit. She examined the cleanliness of the car and then said something to Lolo, our sometimes driver and the man who had just washed it, and he quickly skipped over to open the gate. He always hurried when she asked him to do something—I think more out of respect than urgency. I hated watching him run like this. It made him seem a lot younger than his white beard suggested. But my mother always watched him with a look of contentment, satisfied, I suspect, that she was being obeyed.

She got into the driver's seat, rolled down the window and yelled up at me. "Stop gawking at the neighbours. You're making us look envious."

Then she put on her sunglasses, reversed the big red Mercedes and drove out past Lolo, who stood holding the gate open. I had jumped away from the window at her instruction and worried about whether the boys knew that I had been looking at them. I ran to the bathroom to check on my hair, put on lipgloss, and took a minute to decide if my skirt was too short. I heard my brother's voice, which carried from the area between the house and the back room up to the bathroom window.

He said, "*Ma'gents*," which was how he and his friends greeted each other. Someone said "Heita!" and then the voices faded with their footsteps as they walked up to the gate. My parents had put in lots of pretty grey pebbles on the walk so that you always heard people's footsteps coming and going—a sound I had always found reassuring until years later on the day it became terrifying to me.

I ran down the stairs, but before I could see who they were the six tall boys disappeared from sight.

The rest of the story I have heard from my brother. The short version is that someone—he can't remember who—had suggested that they go and catch a football game in Kasi. Someone's brother was playing, and Basi and his friends could pay to join and play for money. They had searched their pockets and found some money, added it up and calculated that if they doubled it in the game they could buy four *diphatlho*, a township delicacy that makes for a filling meal.

They were running as fast as they could through the woods leading to the main road in order to catch the game, when one of them almost tripped over a woman's decomposing body, covered in maggots; nearby, a blood-stained white shoe could be seen under a bush. There was nothing else around but the clothes on her body.

At first the boys ran away. But then, one by one, they walked back to look, both horrified and fascinated. They then continued through the woods and across the road, and managed to reach the street where the game had been, not caring about playing and having lost their appetites, but excited to tell an eager audience of other young men about the body.

They were thirteen years old and I was nine.

"She's no one. She's from down there," my brother often told me.

It was four years later and we still had no idea whose body it had been, but I had held on to my brother and his friends' find obsessively—the way another child might hold on to a favourite fairy tale.

Basi used to say, whenever I brought it up, "You mustn't be grim."

I had had a lot of sleepless nights after I first heard about it, wondering whose family she belonged to, who was looking for her (if anyone) and what had taken her there. I dreamed about her, putting many faces to a body that I had never even seen. Basi and I also spent many afternoons in the back room talking about her. I remember clearly how those afternoons would go: I would be sitting with my back against the wall, hugging my legs and asking questions, and he would be feeding me details as easily as if he were reading from a script. I was like a dog taking scraps from a child who didn't want his food.

One of these times was a particular Thursday afternoon, the day before a social at Basi's school. Even before my parents had agreed to let me go I had lain in bed making mental images of the clothes in my wardrobe, deciding what would go well together. I had bought new shoes and I had plans to go to the salon, which was not unusual because this was something my mother, my brother, and I did every week.

Now, I have to say that I was one of those girls who had always been aware of boys. Remember earlier when I said I had checked my skirt and put on lipgloss before going outside to see my brother's friends? That had been me from the time I was in crèche. Whenever my brother brought his friends home I would spend time in front of the mirror—just a little less time than I spent before going to school. I brushed my hair this way and that. I put on this dress, and then took it off to wear jeans, and then took them off to try a skirt, and then took that off and went back to the dress before deciding that the jeans were better. I know a lot of people only start this when they reach puberty, but I had been in front of that mirror and thinking about boys for as long as I can remember.

My friend Olebogeng—or as we called her, Ole—was different in that way. She didn't understand what she called my "boy craze." She would sit on my bed watching me change in and out of clothes, obsessively focussed on my hair, and we'd have variations of the same conversation.

She'd start with something like, "I don't see what you see in so-and-so" (the name of the boy I'd been talking about all month long). "Honestly," she'd say pulling her Dobbs hat further down her forehead, "boys *bore* me."

I would look at her not-tight-enough jeans and her T-shirt (*T-shirt!*) and say, "Ole, I don't understand. You never wear skirts, you never wear dresses and you complain about boys boring you."

"My mother says the same thing: 'They might notice you if you wore a skirt.' Really," she'd pick up a book, prop her feet up on the desk and, reclining on the chair, add, "wearing skirts would just encourage them."

"Yes!" I'd laugh as I walked around in my bra, looking for a tighter blouse. "That's the idea, duh!"

We would sit secretly at the window, looking out at the quiet road to make sure my mother didn't find us blowing smoke out of her house.

"Boys are only fun as friends," Ole would say. Then she'd look me up and down and add something like, "That bra doesn't look comfortable *at all*. It has *wires* underneath. I'm happy with a sports bra. You should try them."

"Just for sports, Ole," I'd blow. "For. Sports." I'd shake my head and watch her in wonder.

Boys are only fun as friends. Ole's favourite words.

4

SO THERE I WAS, about two months before I turned fourteen, obsessed with the usual things (my hair, my clothes, the dead woman in the woods) as well as some new things (the school social and Vera-the-Ghost—I'll get back to her later). It was the end of March and the season was changing. The air had lost its warmth and the earth looked barren; the colours of the trees had gone from bright greens to dry, ashen tones.

Basi and I were sitting silently in the back room.

The day before, two significant things had happened. The first was that at my brother's urging, my parents finally agreed to let me go to my first social. We were at the table eating supper when I made yet another desperate attempt to convince them. I had been relentlessly begging for permission for four weeks, ever since I heard about the social.

My mother had set the table beautifully, as always: the cutlery in the right place, the plates and glasses—"These are the most expensive wine glasses; you can tell by their weight"—set perfectly atop a white tablecloth with red flowers, red being my mother's favourite colour. Even with a helper around, my mother preferred to set the table herself. She took special pleasure in having everything *just right*.

"Everyone's going," I was saying.

"Your elbows should never be on the table," said my mother as she picked up a glass of wine, holding it delicately by its stem ("This is how you hold a glass properly"). Her eyes peered at me reprovingly from behind the rim of her glass. Her long and perfectly separated eyelashes rising.

"Sorry." I pulled off my elbows and tucked them behind my back, shoulders pushed back in an effort to help my case.

"Why are you so excited to go and be around boys, Nedi?" said my mother looking down at her food as if she were talking to her plate and not me. "What is this? Adolescence?" She placed the glass down and smoothed the tablecloth with her long fingers. You could see her maroon nail polish glistening in the bright dining-room light. "Hmph!" she said, shaking her head.

Basi was quickly making his way through his second serving of potatoes. He was sitting up straight, his broad shoulders spread across the back of the tall wooden chair. He picked up a serviette from his lap and dabbed it perfectly at the corners of his mouth.

"Basi, you're a perfect gentleman," she said in English with a wide grin.

My father turned the page and read more of his paper.

"My friends will be there," I persisted. "Papa?"

He turned another page, cleared his throat.

"I don't think so, Nana." My father called me Nana whether he was sad, happy, or angry.

At that time Aus'Tselane was working for us. We were losing helpers at a steady rate that year—four people had already been dismissed by our mother for various reasons, which mostly boiled down to their inability to make our house as spotless as the one my mother had grown up in. She would say, "She only polished the floors once this week and not twice," or, "I don't understand why she doesn't use the outside toilet every time," and within weeks the woman would be sent back to her home—usually a small village in the north.

So Aus'Tselane came in and picked up the dishes from our second course. I watched her long arms moving slowly and carefully as she collected each plate. I noticed the safety pins under her armpits neatly holding her dress together.

"Please? Please can I go?" I whined again, slumping forward.

My mother's attention had shifted to Aus'Tselane. She leaned back in her chair and smoothed the table again with her perfectly manicured right hand. Basi was reading something at the back of our father's newspaper.

"I—"

"Shhh, Naledi!" my mother interrupted. "Can we eat in peace, *tu*? Do you know how long it took me to prepare this meal and set the table? After the day I had? *Tu* . . . " Her voice trailed off and she pursed her lips as she watched Aus'Tselane come back with our sweets—glass bowls of custard and jelly on a long red tray. You could see she was taking special care not to let the tray fall.

My mother said, "Tselane, you can have the rest, *nè*?" and Aus'Tselane gave her a long, slow, and graceful nod, so that it looked like she was attempting a bow. When she walked back out of the room she held the tray close to her chest and hugged it with both hands, which made Mama frown in disapproval.

Finally my father folded his newspaper into many small rectangles and placed it to the left of his bowl. He put his hand on top of the paper thoughtfully, as if steadying himself for his next move. He always did give full attention to his sweets. He was the type of man who would eat through a plate of pap and vleis without once glancing at what went into his mouth, but when the ice cream or custard and jelly came he'd put everything down and concentrate only on his bowl.

"Mmm," he said, as always, his lips folded, the tip of his tongue licking. "Mmm," was all he could manage.

"Papa—" I began again.

"Basi, will you be going?" he said, without looking up from his bowl, and my brother politely answered, "*Eeng.*"

After a pause—me holding my breath and kicking his feet

under the table—Basi said, "You know I can watch her. I know all the boys at my school. They're my friends," he added, and I thought: *Nice touch.*

"That's it then," Papa said. "Watch out for your sister. *Heh!* With those eyes." His eyes met mine as he smiled. "I don't want any of those boys anywhere near my Nedi, OK?" He laughed, reaching out to pat my shoulder gently.

My mother frowned again and said, "Stay away from boys, Naledi. You're too young. *Lege ba re eng.* At your age I would never have gone out at night to a place full of boys. Mammy would never have allowed it."

So that was how I ended up going to the social.

The second significant thing that happened that day was that my parents saw Vera. Or, as everyone called her, Vera-the-Ghost. Vera was a tall woman who would have been in her late twenties if she had actually been alive, who was said to run along the edge of the main road at night stopping traffic, her clothes torn, her arms bare and skinny. If you stopped to help, they said, she would come banging on your window and beg for a lift home. With her standing so close, her face only inches from you, you would see that she was crying. "Sobbing like a small child or a woman in mourning," people said.

My parents agreed.

"Her clothes were torn," my mother told us the morning after they had seen her, as we were eating breakfast before school. "There was blood on her blouse."

I shuddered in my school uniform as I sat there trying to chew the spoonful of cereal now dry in my mouth.

"She wore a skimpy little denim miniskirt," she said. "And she was holding one of her shoes in one hand. Just waving it in the air furiously, like she was trying to tell us something."

My father was reading his morning paper as he stood near the sink, but he lowered the paper. He spoke slowly, his voice soft and sad. "She just ran into the middle of the road. Just like that." He stared at the floor in front of him. "I almost hit her with my car."

No one said a word for a minute. We all looked down, at our plates, picturing the scene.

"How did you know it was her?" Basi asked thoughtfully.

"Well," my father said as he folded the paper, composing himself. "My hair . . . stood on end."

My mother said, "And my skin felt taut."

"And then she was gone." He snapped his fingers. "I said, 'Climb in and I'll take you home,' but she was gone."

"Just as suddenly as she had come," said my mother. "It was my first time seeing her and really, I'm telling you . . . " Her voice trailed off and she shuddered visibly, like it was all happening again.

People spoke about Vera-the-Ghost with such concern that one was always left desperately sad after hearing the story. I remembered how the year before I had been at Ole's house when her parents told us about Vera. Ole's mother was folding a blanket after doing the washing. She stood there with it clutched to her chest, shaking her head in disbelief. "Ai!" she said miserably. "*Mara, whose* child is she?"

So that Thursday afternoon after my parents had told us about seeing Vera, I was speaking to Basi in the back room, my voice shaking.

"Those woods," I told him. "They hold secrets."

He looked up at me, knowing what was coming.

"I mean, we still don't know whose body it was that you found that year."

"She's no one," he said again, waving his hand as if to swat away the question. "No one named her. No one came looking for her. She may not even have been from here. She may have been . . . "

I waited as he leaned forward to pick out a tape and compare it to a CD. Often when we spoke about the body, my brother had his mind on something else. The body had held its intrigue in *my* mind, but with him . . . well, he was hardly interested any more.

"May have been what?" I tried.

"*Heh?*" he said, searching my face to remind him what we had been talking about. "Oh," he continued nonchalantly. "She may—" He lifted the tape, suddenly excited. "Here it is!"

"Basi!"

"Ja? Oh. She may have been, I don't know . . . *letagwa.*"

This didn't make me feel better. Maybe she had been a drunkard living on the street. Maybe. It seemed to help Basi dismiss her, but the story didn't haunt me any less.

Basi casually flipped through the tapes neatly organized in a long red tin box that he kept in the back room. His fingers moved as if he were demonstrating a slow walk, one finger after the other across the tapes—occasionally pausing as he considered which one to use for the mix he was making. He did not look up at me; his eyes narrowed the way they did when he was doing his maths homework.

With his hands still holding the box, he hooked his foot around the leg of his chair and pulled himself closer to the bed. He took off his shoes before putting his feet up on the bed, as if our mother were watching him. Clearing his throat, he stared down at his watch and glanced quickly outside before he resumed flipping through the tape stack. He was waiting for Kgosi, and I clung to the last few minutes I had with him. When he was out with Kgosi, only hunger pangs would bring him home.

I pulled my knees closer to my chest and pushed my back harder against the freshly painted wall, because this topic always made me shiver.

"She must belong to a family," I said.

"No one claimed her," he replied flatly and shrugged, pulling out a tape and placing it in the boom box. "There was nothing left of her. She *rotted*."

The picture I imagined, that of maggots and decaying flesh, made me gag. I pushed my face towards the window and breathed in the fresh air.

Outside, the sun was a large red ball sinking in the distance, making the room darker as it disappeared.

"It's horrible," I said. "I read somewhere that serial killers sometimes wait years and years before they strike again. What if that person, the person who killed her—"

Then Basi was patiently saying, "Nedi, Nedi, Nedi," and his chair was shifting towards me. Placing his hand gently on my leg, he said slowly, "Just do what I do. Forget it." He looked into my eyes for a long while until I nodded.

Then he pushed his chair back, propped his feet back up on the bed and, holding up a white tape, casually asked, "Arthur?"

I lifted my chin from my knees. "With Luther? I don't think so. How do you mix kwaito with R&B?"

"You're right," he said, putting the tape back in the box. He looked at me and grinned. "You're absolutely right."

As if he were remembering something he added, "If you get this scared, then I can't tell you other things boys see when they go through the woods . . . "

He looked up at the freshly painted ceiling and the new ceiling fan. I could sense he was drifting off and he was sad, and I understood that we were changing the subject, that I needed to let it go.

"*Saw*," he said.

"What?" I asked, confused.

"Saw. In the past. When we used to go through the woods . . . back in the day."

I shook my head and patted him on the back the way one of his friends would. "You still see them," I said gently.

He gave a deep sigh and glanced at his watch.

I said, "Kgosi's coming soon?"

At this he smiled before standing up and going to open the door. As the draught moved in I heard slow footsteps on the pebbles outside, and knew that to be Kgosi's suave stride. I knew our time together had come to an end.

5

I HAD A BATH to get ready for the social, opened the windows so the steam would not flatten my hair, and scrubbed my face with a fruit-flavoured face wash. Afterwards, in my room, I stopped to notice the silence. Life around the house had come to a standstill, the calm of it almost lulling me to sleep, like hearing jazz or the blues after a big lunch on a Sunday afternoon.

My mother was at the shop helping my father close up, my brother was in his room getting ready—or so I thought, because his music was drifting softly from under his door—and Aus' Tselane was listening to a Sesotho radio talk show, which was occasionally interrupted by some soft and slow music. From the outside room where she slept, the music blew in through my window with the cool evening breeze.

Up on the hill, in *di*Ex, life was calmer than it was past the main road, after you crossed the woods. We were not in the suburbs, where things were always quiet and people ignored their neighbours, but we were close enough, and everyone did their best to make it feel like we were not in Kasi. There were walls surrounding homes and these walls were very high so that the average person walking past was not able to see into the yard. Sometimes you didn't even see the bottom half of the house; sometimes you only saw the roofs.

You had to get used to hardly ever seeing your neighbours except when they drove out in their cars. There were cameras at some people's gates and intercom systems so that

every guest was announced before entering—which elimi-
nated hawkers and the friendly neighbour who decided to
come in on a whim. And, unlike in Kasi, most children played
in their backyards instead of in the street. That, or they were
indoors watching American comedy shows in English. Since
you rarely saw or spoke to people around you, you knew your
neighbours only by reputation: the lawyer who was the second
youngest person ever imprisoned at Robben Island; the doctor
who worked in the location's first private hospital; the famous
model; the owner of every bakery we knew. And then my
father: the owner of the biggest and oldest supermarket in the
location.

Although we never heard the noise from Kasi my mother
would still point out, "We're not far enough. The dust from
Down There still makes its way up in August." Down There or
At the Bottom was another way we referred to the old houses.
Or sometimes we'd say "*ko motseng.*"

I had many such moments of stillness in my room. I recalled
that when I was younger and we lived down in the location,
people would drift in and out of our house, coming by just to
say hi or to borrow something or share some gossip. If someone
had a party it might go on all weekend so that you were
listening to the same tape over and over and over again, all day,
all night, all weekend. If there was a fight at the party, or just on
the street, you'd drop whatever you were doing to run outside
and see what was going on. There were times when people
didn't finish getting dressed—men without shirts, women
covering their bodies with a large shawl or blanket—because
they'd had to hurry outside in case they missed something.

I would get quite nostalgic at these moments, thinking of
the friends I didn't see so often any more, or wishing someone
would drift in and ask me what time the social started, what
time was I leaving, and that they hoped I had a good time or

I should come to their house the next day and tell them all about it. I wore my new short miniskirt with the zipper on the side. My hair was perfectly curled with hot hair tongs, my blouse was red and black, and my shoes had heels—which would have made one or two teachers at my own school faint, but I was having fun. I applied my mother's lipstick carefully and dabbed it with my little finger. I smoothed my skirt down with both palms and I combed my hair lightly for what must have been the tenth time. And then, very, very carefully, I sat in front of the mirror and hoped this wouldn't crease my skirt. I threw my shoulders back and pushed my breasts forward—they were quite big at thirteen and *oh!* how perfect they looked in that blouse.

I thought of Ole, who sometimes came into my room when I was getting dressed and watched me in wonder. The last time she had sat on my bed poking at her breasts and saying with a sigh, "Don't you wish they'd take their time growing?" I had laughed and said that I didn't mind.

Now I imagined that she was down in Kasi, probably playing snakes and ladders or Monopoly with some boys at a corner shop. She had scoffed at the idea of going to the social. "I hate those boys at your brother's school," she had said. "They're so irritating."

I turned around to look at the bed, wishing I could share my excitement with someone. But I caught a glimpse of the time on the clock at the side of my bed and jumped.

As always happened when I was getting dressed—and without warning—my mind had become restless and I'd lost track of time. Basi joked about it. He'd smile and say in English, "I love how you dream for hours and then you're shocked at how time flies."

I stood up, re-examined the size of my bum and wished, as always, that it were smaller. I checked my hair and nails and shoes again. Then I said to the girl in the mirror, while imagining I was talking to a boy, "I'm Naledi." I sucked in the corners of my lower lip and liked the look of it. Then I smiled to myself, wondering about the many cute boys who were now at their homes getting ready and what they would think of my short skirt and my curled hair, and I grinned at the mirror, giddy with anticipation.

When my mother arrived she stayed in her car and waited for me and Basi. I knew she was impatient, ready to get on with it. Mama's mind was always busy: deciding what the shop needed, what the house needed, what my father and Basi needed and what I should be doing better. But I was glad she didn't come in because the distance between our house and my brother's school stretched longer every minute I spent in the house. So it was with sheer glee that I ran downstairs, feeling like I was leaping into the most important and exciting night of my life.

When I burst out through the front door Mama stuck her head through the car window and said, "Where's Basi?"

"Does my hair look OK?"

She paused and looked me up and down, frowning at first and then smiling faintly. "Is that my lipstick?"

I said nothing.

"Yes, you look fine . . . Where's Basi?"

"In his room, I think." I had my hand on the car door when I realized that I had only assumed he had been in his room. I hadn't actually seen him or heard his footsteps in a long time. Though his music was still on.

My mother, very irritably, said, "I saw a group of his friends at the bottom and I looked but didn't see him. They were shuffling around when they saw me, like they were trying to hide something." Here she clicked her tongue angrily.

"They're scared of you," I said, trying to calm her. She liked people being afraid of her.

"I know," she said, shaking her head distractedly. "They always seem to be hiding something from me."

I knew right away that my brother must have disappeared down the hill some time between me being in the bath and me getting dressed, and I was quite stunned that he had not calculated the time well enough to make sure he would be back before Mama got home. That alone made me think that something was seriously amiss. My brother and his friends had inner alarm clocks. They moved through life without watches but managed to time everything in their heads and get it right without fault. In fact, when Basi received a watch for his sixteenth birthday he had worn it for a day or two before telling me, "Don't tell Papa, but I can't deal with this thing. It messes with my head."

"Eish!" I said, thinking quickly. "Ah, I forgot. He wanted a tape for tonight—he promised the DJ he would bring him the new Brenda tape and I think he went to get it from Kgosi." I tried to sound carefree but I hardly ever can when telling lies.

Then I pulled down the mirror above the passenger seat so that I didn't have to look at Mama. I fidget when I'm nervous.

She sucked her teeth. I smoothed my hair. The sucking of the teeth let me know that her store of patience was dropping, and I fidgeted some more—fixing my hair, rubbing the tips of my nails, pulling at my clothes.

Just as we were ready to turn the corner, our eyes peeled as we searched the road for signs of him, there came Basi striding casually up the road. Surprisingly he was with Kgosi, even though Kgosi was not coming to the social.

My mother hooted in three short bursts: be-beep-beep! But Basi and Kgosi, instead of parting immediately, stopped to say something to each other.

Again my mother sucked her teeth, and I pulled at the hem of my skirt.

Now I was getting frustrated with my brother, who was making us late and making my mother angry and all in all ruining the beginning of my first big night.

Kgosi and Basi spoke like two conspiring businessmen these days. They would shove their hands in their pockets, their heads close together; they would each speak in a low voice, the other nodding furiously.

For as long as I could remember my brother and his friends had talked about cars: cars they admired, cars they wished they could have, cars other people had, and cars they were going to buy someday. Then they went to high school and all they could talk about were girls, in exactly the same way as they had talked about cars: girls they admired, girls they wished they could have, girls other people had, girls they were going to have someday.

I watched Kgosi and Basi and felt a now familiar tightening of my stomach, wishing I could make Kgosi leave. Whenever Kgosi came to our house, Basi acted as if he wanted me to go away, and when I didn't, they would leave instead. So now there they were, with their backs turned away from us, as though they were unaware of us.

When my mother pressed the base of her palm against the hooter again, the sound came out longer and louder: beeeeeeeeeeeeeeeeeeep! Which had the boys finally doing their strange handshake—some odd hand-holding, thumb-pressing and prolonged pulling of fingers. Kgosi then turned around and disappeared down the road without even glancing in our direction.

Basi ran towards the car and I stepped out of the front seat as I always did. When we met briefly between the two open doors I said softly but irritably, "*Ayeye*," which means, "You're in trouble," and he winked at me, happy as a clown. It always had the effect of making me feel both reassured and silly.

This was and still is Basi: he moves through the world calmly and smoothly, making it all look so easy and fun. When we were growing up it made me and everyone around him look overzealous. You always felt you needed to calm down around Basi—and even more around Kgosi. They'd throw you a wink or one of their confident smiles and you'd think: *I need to get sorted.*

As soon as he climbed in he said, easy as a summer breeze, "Sorry, Ma."

Mama didn't say anything. She pressed her foot quite forcefully against the accelerator and if we had been on the unpaved roads further down the hill we would have left a cloud of dust behind us.

Once we were on the main road she said, "Is his mother still in prison?"

This was something Mama brought up every time she saw Kgosi. Whenever she said it, Basi would take a deep breath and pause, gathering his thoughts before nodding easily.

"How much longer?" she asked, now sounding much calmer.

We were almost out of the location, the car going towards the highway. Fruit sellers along the road were packing up their stock—slowly, in case anyone wanted to stop and buy something at the last minute. When we came to a set of robots, a woman with a child wrapped in a blanket around her steadily stood up from the ground, her feet wide apart and one arm holding the baby on her back. The child had tears streaming down her cheeks. Her mother unwrapped the blanket and pulled her close to her breast, stroking her head gently.

I watched and wondered why I wanted to know them. My mother's voice pulled me back into the car.

"How much longer will she be in there?" she was saying again—not actually asking. "They'll never let her out. Women like her make allies in there. She probably isn't behaving."

Basi fiddled with the radio without engaging.

"They bond in there!" Mama's voice competed with the sound of the radio. "There are so many of them who've done what she's done, that they just bond in there like the criminals they are. *Heh! Waitse*, I remember Nono from the time we were little girls."

The song "One Love" came on. Mama's fingers wrapped more tightly around the steering wheel.

Let's. Get. Together, and feeeel all right.

And then a man's voice, with an English-Afrikaans accent, said: *The time is now* . . . And then it was Cyndi Lauper singing: *Time after time, time after time, time after* . . . The quicker Basi's fingers moved the knob, the louder Mama's voice rose.

I didn't like it when Basi was upset. He went completely silent.

"What she did shocked everyone, but I wasn't surprised. I wasn't even a little bit surprised."

Pepsi Cola— . . . *It is now sunny and mild in Pret*— . . . *Two men in the East Rand were found guilty of*—

Basi turned off the radio and rubbed his hands together as if to warm them.

"*Ka nnete*, Basi." Mama sighed with relief and slowed herself down. "This is not the type of family you should be around. You have a lot more to lose if something happens."

I looked at her, confused.

"Like what?" Basi said sharply, turning his head to Mama.

She was taken aback by the abruptness of his tone. From my seat in the back I saw her head shake and her hands rub the steering wheel up and down.

After another deep sigh, she said, "I'm not saying anything would happen. But look what kind of mother he has . . . I don't think he's capable of . . . Well, I don't think he has good role models." She took another deep breath. "I don't think he has good role models. That's all."

Basi's hands went around his headrest and then tugged at his seatbelt.

Oh no, I thought.

"Kgosi is the *most* decent guy in the world," Basi finally said, forcefully, in English. "The absolute, *most* decent guy you'll ever meet," he continued. "He's a solid guy. A *solid* guy!" If he had been inclined to raise his voice he would have, but he didn't. Basi's voice tended to go lower the angrier he got.

Mama sighed and shrugged. "I just don't want anything to happen to you," she said softly, a bit rattled. Here she reached out and rubbed his cheek.

My mother was always affectionate with Basi when they were in disagreement.

I couldn't look.

My eyes wandered to the scenes outside. There was the big shopping centre that was going up. Next to it was the old one that was being torn down. There was the new suburb, the one most boys from his school lived in. There was the bridge with graffiti that said: *Stop the Gravy Train.* There was a White man holding close to his chest a sign that said: *Twee kinders. Geen kos.* Two children. No food.

"I would give him money for food if he would work for me," Mama said. "But he would rather die than work for me."

In a few minutes I would be arriving at my first social and hopefully meeting my first boyfriend. And then, finally, there we were at Basi's school. We could hear the music in the hall as we drove in.

It was dark in the car park and the only brightness came from the entrance to the hall. In the dimness outside I recognized a few people. There was Lesedi, a friend from school, with a skirt that was even shorter than mine and her hair in a tight ponytail. There was Marjorie, all legs and long blonde hair, talking to Jason—also all long legs with blonde hair—on the steps going up to the hall entrance. When our car stopped I jumped out and slammed the door in my excitement, then turned to use the car window as my mirror.

Basi waved to a group of boys who were standing and laughing at a distance. Two girls I didn't recognize walked past our car and said, "Hey, Basi."

With a broad smile and his hands in his pockets, looking like he owned the car he was now leaning on, he said, "Hey," which had them giggling as they walked off.

I turned around to search for my friends and when my name was called from two directions I first turned to the one that was coming from our car.

"O itshware pila," was what my mother said before starting the engine. To Basi she said, shaking her head, "Only pick one girl. They're already lining up." She laughed at her own joke, then she started to manoeuvre the car through the crowds of the excited and heavily made-up girls she was referring to.

"Basi!" I called out to my brother and held on to his sleeve.

"I know," he said. "Mom's going crazy." Basi always called her "Mom" when we were around his friends from school. Never around Kgosi or any of his other Kasi friends—around them she was "my ou lady" or "Setswadi."

"Heh?"

"You saw how she was. Kgosi and his mom and all of that?"

"Basi, how do I look?"

"I mean, can you believe that?" But he was distracted and walking away, waving at people all along the way.

"Ba-si!" I said through clenched teeth. "How. Do. I. Look?"

My two best friends—Kelelo and Limakatso, girls from school—came and stood with us. Both staring at him like he was a beautiful sunset.

"Haaaaaaaaai Basi," they said in unison.

"Hey girls," he said smoothly in a soft voice I didn't recognize. I looked from them to him in wonder. How was it that every girl I knew—except Ole—thought my brother was, as they said, "Too bloody cute"?

He must have seen the look on my face because he put his arm over my shoulder and then, with a kiss on my forehead, said, "You look stunning, Nedi." Which didn't count because his eyes were already across the rugby field looking at another group of girls.

I smiled anyway.

He looked back at my friends. "You girls—sorry, I mean ladies—look beautiful. Really." He ran his eyes up and down each one. And with a kiss on the tips of his fingers he said, "Really, you're all beauts," a word all the boys at his school used just about every two minutes.

"He's *such* a gentleman!" they cooed as he walked away.

I rolled my eyes.

"He's being strange," I said. "When we get home he'll for sure be staring at his maths homework like it's *for sure* the love of his life."

"Oh my gosh! That's, like, the cutest thing in the world!" Limakatso was using her there-are-boys-around voice, which was nasal and involved saying "like" all the time.

"Shall we go in?" Kelelo's way of speaking at these times involved incessant questioning (as in: "Shall we talk to those boys?" "Shall I dance with him?" and "Shall I ask him his name for you?") while "for sure" was my contribution to the language we used around boys.

Going up the steps was a challenge, since the boys from the school stood there examining us as if deciding which one to pick for their prize. We tried to hold back our giggles while hoping not to fall and trying to look like we were perfectly comfortable in our short skirts.

When we walked through the large open doors of the school's main hall it was into throngs of guys and girls chatting, laughing, putting arms around one another. It felt as if we had walked into a free and forbidden world, a place teenagers dream of and parents dread. I saw a boy pull a girl, their hands in each other's back pockets, and a couple in a corner with bodies pressed against each other, the boy kissing the girl's neck. All I could think was that I wanted to be at each and every coming social for the rest of my school days . . . and I never wanted to go home.

My friends and I were first separated by Limakatso's boyfriend, who took her to the centre of the hall to slow dance beneath disco balls and dimmed lights. Kelelo and I stood waiting at the edge of the hall, trying not to look too hopeful.

Basi was standing near the door chatting with a boy I immediately recognized—because although I had tried not to look like I was searching for someone, I had been hoping to see him from the moment I had heard about the social. He looked in our direction and if the room had been brighter I might have seen whether he was smiling or not. Soon he left the hall and so did Basi.

A boy called Neo came up and put his arm around Kelelo and pulled her to the dance floor. He didn't speak to her, just smiled in a self-assured way that I didn't like, though it didn't stop me from being envious. So, afraid of standing alone in a dark room full of couples dancing and whispering into each other's ears, I moved swiftly and walked through the door.

There, facing the door, was my brother talking with his friends Moabi and Kitsano and two other boys. I didn't know where to look, but they were right in front of me, so I had to go towards them, trying not to smile too broadly. I felt as if they were all watching my every step, and I had never felt so exposed and uncomfortable in my life. I wondered if my lipstick was smudged, or if I had any on my teeth, if my hair was flat, if my breath was fresh and if my skirt was too short, and felt my back suddenly get very warm.

But Basi moved towards me with a wink and put my arm in his, patting it as we walked towards his friends.

"Gentlemen," he said with mock gravity. "My sister, Naledi."

Moabi smiled at me.

"Nice to meet you, Miss Naledi." And then he laughed and I sort of laughed. A bit. I couldn't relax. I felt Kitsano's eyes on me and couldn't look in his direction.

"Nice to meet you," Kitsano said, slowly. His smile was guarded. I thought he seemed more shy than I had imagined. He said nothing else, so I stood there making small talk with my brother and his friends, hoping for something to happen to me that I could talk about at school on Monday morning.

So when Kitsano—the tall boy with smooth, light skin and a clean-shaven head—touched my left breast a bit later that night, cupped it and wildly rubbed my thigh, I thought: *I'm so glad I'm wearing my favourite red bra.* And also: *Am I supposed to pull my tongue back or stick it out the way he's doing in my mouth?*

The darkness behind the school's main hall gave you privacy, even though you could see the outlines of other teenage bodies pressed together in the distance and were wondering, if they looked up and saw you, would they recognize you? Would you want them to, or not? I didn't mind if, on Monday, everyone talked about me being Kitsano's girlfriend. He was so cute and he wasn't a prick at all, by private school standards. I had never seen him talking to more than one girl at a time, unlike my brother and his other friends, who always had a large female audience. And I didn't remember ever hearing about him standing up a girl, or kissing her and telling everyone about it.

I had had my eye on Kitsano for a long time. He was the new boy from Botswana whose parents were diplomats in South

Africa. I had seen him for the first time a few weeks before, when he'd played hockey with Basi against Boys' High. I'd liked him right away because he was new and not one of the ones all the girls in my school were already talking about. He was also so cute, I thought, and so quiet that when I said hi to him after another match—having been dared to by Limakatso, who was sick of me talking about him without actually knowing him—he smiled a broad, pearly white smile and winked instead of speaking, and I was smitten.

Now here he was, sitting next to me, cupping my breast and kissing me furiously. I didn't know what Ole was so sceptical about. I didn't find boys boring at all.

When Basi called my name, I was embarrassed but more annoyed.

"Mama's here," his voice rang out from somewhere in the distance.

When I looked up his back was turned to us and his hand was raised, gesturing towards the front of the building. I stood up and so did Kitsano. Not knowing how to look him in the eye I straightened my skirt and stared at my shoes.

"Can I call you?" he mumbled and cleared his throat.

"Yes." I grinned. I turned around and walked away.

"What . . . Where were you and *who* were you with?!" my mother's voice roared from the front seat as soon as I had closed the door.

I didn't say anything.

"I hope . . . I *really* hope you were not with a boy," she said. Her body was turned towards me. When I steeled myself to glance at her I saw the look of disgust on her face.

"Well," Basi said slowly, with a slight laugh, "she might have been, if she hadn't spent so much time with her girls." He turned around casually and smiled at me. "What do you girls talk about anyway?"

Mama looked from me to him. "She wasn't with a boy?"

He shook his head and laughed again, as if her question amused him greatly. Then he turned around and pulled down the mirror in the passenger-seat visor, eyeing me in its reflection. "Ja, sure. Nedi, it's a social because you're supposed to *socialize* . . . you know, with people you *don't* know?"

Mama straightened up and turned on the car. Basi shook his head.

Then, as if he had just remembered something, he added, "We put a lot of effort into this thing. The least the girls could do is stop huddling together in the toilets doing their lipstick and giggling . . . I just may not take you any more." His voice was teasing.

Mama kept driving and said nothing for a while. And then: "I'm glad you were there to watch her."

6

NOZIPHO JACQUELINE NOKANE, also known as Nono, was born Jacqueline Nozipho Maseko in Atteridgeville, Pretoria, which is also known as Phelindaba or just Pheli to its locals. She got married to Moitshepi Raymond "Speed" Nokane in the firestorm that followed the massive 1980 Sasol bombing in the Orange Free State. They say Bra Speed, as he was known to all of us, came to his wedding black and blue and bold-faced, wearing a perfectly tailored suit to go with the large bandage circling his head and the swollen lip, the dried blood, and the stitches that ran the length of his left cheek. He looked straight ahead out of his right eye, the only one that was open, and forced the right corner of his mouth into a smile.

Aus' Nono is said to have held her son Kgosi, then only two years old, by the hand and strolled him proudly along as the people sang and danced and *hee-lee-lee*'d up and down the streets. Location history has her looking very happy, calm and satisfied at her own wedding, content to finally have Bra Speed back.

"Tell me your deepest, darkest secret," I asked Ole, a favourite prelude to good conversation between the two of us. We were sitting in our backyard drinking cold Oros and eating Tennis Biscuits from the packet.

"I let Shorty look at my breasts," she said, all blasé.

"What?!" I laughed, almost spitting out my drink.

Ole shrugged. Then she sat up and flung her legs across the

chair, facing me. She was excited. "Then he let me hold his gun. His *gun*!" She grinned and waited for my reaction.

"What . . . with the breasts . . . ?"

"Who cares about that? Boys are stupid. His father has a gun and I wanted to see it. All this time he's been telling me about it. I didn't believe him, so he said, 'Show me your breasts and I'll let you see the gun.' Can you believe that?" Here she slumped back into her chair. "Boys are easy."

"What?! Why would you let him see your breasts? That's special. That's for someone special!"

Ole laughed at me. "Nedi! They're just breasts. Special is for other things. Anyway, the gun was really, really amazing."

I hadn't been counting on this. I had been hoping she would stay on the talk about the breasts.

"Did he touch them?"

"The breasts?" she asked as if we were talking about something else. "No!"

I would have loved not to be talking about guns. I'd rather have talked about boys: boys kissing, boys seeing breasts. Then I would have told her about Kitsano. But here is the thing with Ole: it wasn't so much that she was not interested in boys. She was very interested. In fact, I would say that she was even a bit fascinated with them, although she would never say that. She was just very competitive with them—she could do anything they could, sort of thing. And she was also very interested in guns and war stories. As a result, she liked Shorty, Kgosi's younger brother, Bra Speed's youngest son.

"If I had been old enough," she said, looking wistful, "I would have joined them, *waitse*."

I had heard her say this many times. I brought my glass to my mouth to take a sip and kept it there a while longer so that she wouldn't see my face.

"That's . . . not so wise," I started.

She laughed. "Girls are always scared of guns."

I cleared my throat. "You're a girl too."

"Not like you!"

"OK . . . " I didn't know what to say. The thing about it is, I never did know what to say when she started going on about guns and not being a girl like me. I was never all that interested in guns. She knew that. She was not interested in boys in the same way as I was. I knew that. It was just . . . I knew that any conversation about guns and MK would lead to Bra Speed, and that was not entirely safe ground because it would lead to Aus' Nono and the fact that Aus' Nono (a very close childhood friend of Ole's mother) was in prison. Ole would say "wrongfully" and I would say "not wrongfully." That was touchy.

I didn't mind hearing about Bra Speed. Basi talked about him enough. I knew that he had been in MK. I knew he had been a comrade and that he had gone into hiding many, many times. I also knew that Ole had always lamented being born too late to join MK. What I didn't want to talk about was that Bra Speed was dead because his wife had killed him. I didn't want to talk about that—especially not on this day, when I had such interesting news myself.

I shook my head and took a deep breath.

"Umkhonto—" Ole started.

"My mother hates MK," I told her.

There was silence between us, except for the crunch of the biscuits and the splashing of the mini fountain in the far right corner, the one Mama had installed a year earlier, after she had gone to a party in Waterkloof and admired a large pond and fountain in someone else's yard.

I knew what Ole was thinking and she knew what I was thinking and I wished we could talk about something else. Like the fact that I had been kissed! Ohhhh, Kitsano. Kitsano, Kitsano, Kitsano . . .

But I could feel us getting close to where we would have to talk about Bra Speed and Aus' Nono.

"Anyway!" I started, trying to change the subject.

"Eish! I would have loved that. I would have fought in those times. Do you know how many women left South Africa? How many died for the country?"

My mind wandered. I sipped, I fidgeted, I waited.

"Umkhonto," she continued, "that's where I would have been."

"You could have died!" I said, my voice rising higher than I had intended.

"Bra Speed didn't. Bra Moz didn't." She was referring to a friend of Bra Speed's, one of the best-known cross-border strategists, whom everyone called Moz because of the amount of time he had spent in Mozambique. His Portuguese was apparently impeccable. I had heard this from my brother, who had loved sitting at Bra Speed's feet, taking in everything about MK.

"Yes, but . . . " I said cautiously. "But . . . it was so dangerous. All those men—"

"What?!" She stood up. Ole was always ready for a fight.

I thought: *You would have done well as a comrade.* I sunk into my chair and looked at the fountain. Steadying my voice, I told her, "More men than women survived." This is not a fact, it's just something I had surmised from all the stories Basi had told me.

"*Haua! Haua!*" She slapped her thighs angrily. "That's not true. So many women . . . " She wiped her forehead. "So many women! Where do I start? Mma Lebo, Aus' Joyce . . . " She counted them off one by one with her fingers.

I wished we could talk about Kitsano.

"Eish, Ole! Why are we talking about this? Apartheid is in the past, first of all." I tried not to sound frustrated but I don't think I succeeded. "And anyway . . . and *any*way . . . "

"And anyway what?"

"And anyway, what is it with guns? Someone could get killed."

"I think every woman should know how to use a gun."

I squinted against the sun. "We're fourteen." (I wasn't. But nearly.)

"Better start now," she said, relaxing, taking a sip of Oros and moving her finger around the rim of the glass. Then she put down the glass and leant forward, legs apart, eyes on the ground.

"I think . . . " She cleared her throat. "I think . . . If you see what I've seen, you know. You just know . . . "

I knew what she meant. Living in *di*Ex was not like living on another continent. I knew things. I heard stories.

"You know," I said in agreement. "Like the body?"

"The body . . . Every woman should know how to use a gun," she repeated with more gravity.

I decided to stay away from that one. My mother had told me, "Nozipho wouldn't be in jail with two sons who are living at home without a mother if she had never touched a gun."

Ole, I knew, vehemently disagreed.

We both looked up when we heard the crunch, crunch, crunch of footsteps on the gravel path to the house. Finally Basi and Kgosi turned the corner and, more cheerfully than usual, Basi said, "Heita! Heita!"

He was wearing a new pair of jeans and a crisp white shirt that he mostly saved for weddings, funerals, and those occasions when my mother insisted we wear our best. Kgosi looked handsome in dark blue jeans and a plain, fresh-looking T-shirt.

The two of them moved apart and Basi held out his arm, saying "*Etla!*" to someone we couldn't see yet.

From behind them she slowly stepped forward.

Fingers intertwined with Basi's, her hair so long and straight that it actually billowed like a lace curtain in the breeze. Like a White girl's hair.

She had the biggest, most beautiful eyes I had ever seen, a small and perfectly placed nose, and big, dark, shiny lips that looked like they had lipstick on but didn't. Her white blouse looked both comfortable and sexy. Her earrings caught the sunlight and this, I think, made her eyes sparkle.

She was wearing the blue denim version of a corduroy skirt I had and I started to think that maybe it didn't look quite so stunning on me.

Her eyes looked straight at me. So composed. I noticed that, most interestingly, she didn't look around the way people usually did when they came into our house or yard for the first time. Our house had a shroud of mystery around it: being my father's, being up there, and having tall walls around it. Naturally when people came in for the first time their eyes darted from corner to corner, taking it all in, fascinated. But not her. You would have thought she had been there before and yet I knew that she hadn't. Instead, she looked right into my eyes with only a hint of a smile.

"Hello," she said softly.

Ole and I stood up. One look at Ole and I knew she was thinking the same thing I was.

"Moipone," Ole said and then nervously cleared her throat.

The look on Basi's face was the same as when he had just won a rugby match. His big grin was radiant and animated. This, for reasons I couldn't grasp, irritated me.

"This is my sister," he said. Then, with his hand squeezing hers, he said, "Moipone."

I cleared my throat. Unable to decide on a pose, my arms went from my back to being folded across my chest and then back down.

"Hello," I said to Moipone's eyes.

Ole and I were still staring when Basi, Kgosi, and Moipone

turned to leave, looking like three dancers, the boys on either side of Moipone.

But then Moipone hesitated and turned around as if she had left something behind. When I followed her eyes I saw that, ha! she had noticed the fountain. She examined it curiously— the white stone statue of a child carrying a bowl, with water flowing from it—and then turned her whole body back to face me. To me! As if she was asking me for an explanation. And, understanding her gaze, I shrugged. Then she narrowed her eyes and I saw, or thought I saw, a faint smile, which passed her face so quickly that I wondered if I had imagined it.

Kgosi and Basi had also turned around, but Basi was looking only at her. Kgosi had followed her gaze and was suppressing a laugh, as I've seen him do before while looking at various things at our house: the glass table, the cumbersome wall-to-wall furniture, the colourful picture of a White child sitting in a flowerpot.

When they had gone I realized that I had been holding my breath the whole time.

"She's so pretty," I finally said, with a sigh.

Ole turned, looked me straight in the eye and said, all serious, "She's stunning," spitting out the "t."

We sat down and took a moment to compose ourselves.

"I've never seen her before," I said. "Who is she?"

"She's Moipone," said Ole and took a sip of Oros. "She lives on Kgosi's street. She's new. She and her mother used to live in Block C and her father works in Gauteng."

We were quiet for what felt like a long time until I said, "I think my brother is in love."

As if she had not heard me, Ole said, finally, "Your turn." She reclined in her garden chair. "Tell me your deepest, darkest secret."

"I think I'm in love," I said.

7

MONDAY LUNCH AT SCHOOL. The three of us sat cross-legged in a circle on the grass near the tennis courts, talking about the social.

Finally.

"He put his hands . . . " Limakatso started to say, and then she put her sandwich down and stood to demonstrate, " . . . *all* the way up."

We all broke into fits of giggles.

"Oh. My. Gosh," I said as I tried to hold my breath.

Limakatso was running her hands up her school dress, pulling it up to show more and more of her thighs until we could see her blue panties.

"We can see your panties," Kelelo told her.

"I know!" Limakatso sat down—well, really, she just about fell down. "So could he!"

At this we were rolling on the grass.

When she caught her breath, she said, "But the thing is, where do you put your hands?"

Another fit of laughter.

Kelelo said, bringing her hands around my waist, "I put mine around here. What did you guys do?"

"I put mine on his thighs," I told them.

Their eyes went wide. Kelelo's jaw dropped so that I could see specks of green from her already-swallowed salad.

"That's so naughty!" she said.

"What about her?" I pointed to Limakatso. "He saw her panties!"

Again we fell on the grass, against each other, our legs flailing. *Oh*, I thought, *I'm so excited to finally be talking about this.* I was dreading the moment when the bell would ring. I stretched out on the grass, my head resting on my lunch bag, which I had covered with my school jersey.

"D'you know what else he did?" Limakatso said in a whisper.

"What?" Kelelo and I spoke in unison.

"He touched my boobs," she whispered again excitedly.

I rolled to my side and looked at them. "He touched mine too!" I nearly screamed.

I rested my head on one hand and then tucked my dress between my legs with the other. The Standard One boys were running around a few metres away from us, and I knew they liked to peek out of curiosity. I liked that boys only went up to Standard One at our school. We couldn't have talked like this if boys our age had gone there.

"No. Noooooo," Limakatso said. "I mean, he put his hands inside my dress and actually touched my . . . " Her voice went even lower and she pointed. " . . . My nipples!"

"Oh my goodness," Kelelo said, pressing one hand against her mouth. I tended to be the one who was more easily shocked but that day Kelelo and I were even. I was getting cramps in my stomach from all the laughter.

"Inside?" I asked Limakatso but I was looking at Kelelo.

"*In*side."

Two pairs of small boys' feet suddenly stood next to our food. We looked up to see two seven- or eight-year-olds in khaki school shorts and white shirts staring down at us.

"What?" Limakatso barked at them. "What do you want?"

"Are you talking about kissing?" the taller one said.

"Go away!" all three of us screamed. "Go!"

They ran off, screeching to the rest of their group, "They're talking about kissing! They're talking about kissing!" and some of them started kissing their hands and making kissing noises in our direction.

We rolled our eyes.

"Boys can be so stupid," Kelelo said.

I said, "Remember when we used to think they were gross?" We looked at each other and giggled again.

The bell rang and brought us to our feet. In different corners of the school grounds groups of girls stood up or stopped playing and started moving towards classes. Many of us had our jerseys around our waists and our knee-high socks rolled down. Late autumn in Pretoria is like this and so is winter: it is cold when you go to school but by lunchtime you feel overdressed. The sun is so hot at midday that it may as well be early summer, and then the temperature drops again later. The teachers hated that look though. Girls with their socks rolled down and jerseys around their waists were yelled at for being untidy. So before we reached the classes everyone began straightening their hair, smoothing down their dresses, folding their jerseys neatly and pulling up their socks. I looked around at all the different figures and silently compared them to mine. Bigger bum, stronger legs, nicer breasts.

"I wish I had Mary's legs," Kelelo said as if reading my thoughts. Mary was the star hockey player.

We agreed.

"By the way," Limakatso said as we were rounding the corner, "who is your brother going out with? I didn't see him with anyone at the social and, well, actually—"

"Actually?"

"Actually, my sister asked." Limakatso's sister was at our school. Same age as my brother and, like my brother, also in matric.

We lifted our hands up, palms facing inwards, as we walked

up the stairs. The prefects stood along the old red brick wall at the landing, inspecting the length of our fingernails.

"Your sister likes him?" I was surprised. Limakatso's sister was all about books and sports. The last time I remembered her having a boyfriend she'd been in Standard Eight.

"Single file, please!" one of the prefects yelled from somewhere at the top of the stairs.

I stepped behind Limakatso.

"Matric dance is coming up. I think she wants to ask him."

"Hmmm," I said, intrigued. "I don't think he has a girlfriend."

"Shhhh," another prefect said, glaring, her finger on her mouth.

"If he doesn't have a girlfriend," Limakatso whispered, excited, "then maybe . . . the two of them could even go out."

Then I remembered Moipone and for some reason I had that same sinking feeling I had whenever Kgosi came to our house. That feeling of realizing that I had no time left with Basi.

What was it about her? I wondered.

Basi had been going out with a very pretty girl called Dineo on and off for the previous four years. Whenever they were on, they fell into a pattern: he was always unsure of how long it would last and made little effort to make it last, while she phoned our house all the time wanting to know where he was. Eventually one or the other would get tired of playing their role and they would break up. She was a snob and the kind of girl everyone envied because she was spoiled by her parents and was quite beautiful. My mother liked her very, very much. She invited her to our house a few times, which was unusual because they were hardly looking at marriage. But my mother liked things that made her seem more bourgeois and closer to town. She called it being "modern." She would say, "People should phone and not just drop in. It's more modern," or, "Why is she breastfeeding her child instead of just giving her the bottle? It's not modern," or even, "Send a card to invite people to the party—don't go to their house and ask them in person. Be modern, Nedi."

So she was more than happy with the choice of Dineo, whose parents were lawyers and lived in Waterkloof. Dineo's mother, Tilly, was a friend of my mother's and they spent many hours on the phone talking about what they called their children's love story.

"Wooooo!" she'd exclaim whenever Dineo and Basi were going out again. "You know, Basi and Dineo—those two understand each other. Lovers' spat or not. They sort it out." Then she would giggle with heaps of satisfaction.

For his part, Basi never spoke of Dineo as his girlfriend. He seemed to like being around her. He seemed to like her when he was with her, but he didn't give the impression that he thought of her much when she was gone. On Dineo's visits to our house, in those times when our parents were not home, Basi and Dineo would disappear into his room for what often felt like an entire afternoon. I had come to expect this. They didn't go to the back room where Basi and I often sat and listened to music, or where he would take his friends when they were visiting.

The most Basi would say about Dineo was, "She's . . . open-minded," and, "I like that in a girl."

I only vaguely knew what he meant. Mainly it made me want to be the kind of girl who had qualities that made boys say, "I like that in a girl."

Dineo went to North Girls' High, our sister school, the same one as Ole's. We just called their school North and ours South. Whenever Dineo saw me at a hockey match or a swimming gala, she would call me over to stand with her and her group of friends, grilling me on what my brother had been doing lately.

Basi never asked about her or what she was doing. Instead

he'd laugh, all impressed with the attention she was giving him. "She's hot," he'd say. He said that a lot.

But Moipone? Not even "hot." No mention of her after I met her that first time. He said nothing at all. It was almost as if I had imagined her coming to our house and seeing the nervous and excited look on his face.

"He's kind of . . . I don't know," I told my friends. "I think he's going out with someone but I don't know."

"What do you mean?" Kelelo asked.

I thought about it for a moment. If Basi was going out with Moipone but hadn't said anything about it to me, then maybe he wanted to keep it a secret. Maybe they had just met and he didn't want to spoil it, or maybe, just maybe—this made me feel hopeful—maybe Moipone was actually Kgosi's girlfriend. But that didn't make sense. As soon as I thought it, I knew to let it drop.

I said, before we walked into our class, "No, no. Something is definitely going on with him and someone. He just hasn't told me about it."

"But he tells you everything!" Limakatso said, her eyes wide with disbelief.

My heart sank.

"Ja. I know. He'll tell me soon." I tried to look nonchalant.

"So . . . you don't think my sister should ask?"

"All right, girls!" Mrs Andries's voice bellowed from behind us, a file tucked under her arm and her hands clapping impatiently. "Lunch is over. Be quiet please!"

"I don't know," I whispered as we hurried along. "Yes. Maybe. Probably."

On the days when our driver picked us up from school instead of one of our parents, Basi would run into his room, change out of his uniform and then start walking down the hill. Sometimes he would ask the driver to drive him down to Kasi. But when one of our parents fetched us, they would drive us straight from school to the supermarket, giving him no time to see his friends that day—although sometimes Papa paid Kgosi to work at the shop, and they would see each other that way.

That Monday afternoon I stood outside the school, waiting for one of my parents' cars to arrive. Limakatso and Kelelo had already left, and since the crowds of waiting girls were quickly dispersing, I was getting impatient. When Mama finally arrived, she already had Basi in the front seat and I quickly hopped in the back.

I sensed right away that something was going on because they both looked more cheerful than usual.

Basi turned to me, big grin on his face, and said, "Guess what?"

"What?"

"Your brother is going national!" Mama exclaimed with quick, unrestrained excitement.

"What?!"

"It's not certain," Basi said, putting up his hand. But his own voice rose a little bit when he added, "The coach said I'm on the list."

"The list? What list?" I couldn't control my own overwhelming excitement.

"The list of blokes who are now being looked at—" He slowed himself down, his hand moving up and down as if inserting tangible pauses. He took a deep breath and pushed out his chest, a gesture that made him look very measured. "Who are. Being looked at. For the provincial team."

If I had to give a list of things most important to Basi at that time, it would look like this:

Friends/family

Rugby

School

"Oh. My. Gosh!" I almost jumped out of my seat. "My own brother is a rugby star!"

"No, no." He was pushing the air with his hand again. "We have to wait and see."

"Oh, come on! It's a given. You haven't lost a match!" Here I started counting with my fingers. "Your performance has been consistent. And, oh my gosh! You *are* the team captain. Hello!"

"Heh-heh!" My mother squealed as she drove down the highway back to our home. "Let's celebrate!"

"Ma, there's nothing to celebrate yet. Let's wait. Two weeks." He clasped his hands and I could see—I could really *feel*—how much he wanted this for himself; how much all three of us wanted it for ourselves. The star and the glory.

"*Ngwanake!*" Mama said with emphasis, her voice sounding as if she was choking back tears. She said it with that blend of pride and overwhelmed gratitude we knew so well. "You're on your way . . . I mean, look: the national team only has one Black player! One! With so many of you playing in schools, it's shocking. But . . . you could be . . . "

"Mama," Basi reached his hand out to her shoulder, "First, Chester Williams is Coloured. Second . . . let's wait. Let's wait. Two weeks." And then he said in a whisper to himself, "Two weeks."

Mama sped up to overtake the white bakkie in front of us. As she did, I locked eyes with the man sitting at the back, who smiled and squinted against the wind and the sun. He waved at me and when I raised my hand it was the man sitting next to a dog in front who saw my wave.

Mama clicked her tongue with disapproval.

"You know!" I said.

Mama let out a soft laugh and murmured, "And I know, oh,

a change is goin' come."

Swept up by the mood, Basi switched on the radio and put in a new CD. We sat back in our seats and listened happily to En Vogue sing "Yesterday," each of us with the quiet assurance that Basi's world was growing bigger, coupled with the immense pride that came with that thought.

We hardly said anything else to each other on the long drive home on the highway. We just sat and watched the world go by. My usual relief and calm set in as soon as I saw Silver City. A taxi stopped abruptly in front of us and Mama clicked her tongue. We were almost hit by a PUTCO bus at the first four-way stop, and we almost hit a young girl running carelessly across the road.

"We have a lot of pricing to do today so everyone is very busy. We may have to close the shop late. Get to work as soon as possible."

I liked working at the shop. For a long time when we were younger it had seemed like the centre of the location, and for just as long it had felt like the centre of our world. It had always felt larger than any of us—it being the place where our father went daily, where he spent evenings and weekends and what felt like every waking moment of his life. There were family holidays that he missed because he was at the shop.

A lot had happened there. When it first opened it seemed like everyone in Kasi moved in unison towards it. I remember in the mid-1980s, when I was only a few years old, people standing on its stoep, giving shoppers pamphlets about rallies. There were dance competitions. OMO and Surf promotions happened there. My father's spacious office often served as a last-minute venue for location meetings, and had even been a voters' education station in the year before the 1994 election, when both our parents arranged classes for people who had little understanding of voting.

But our shop's biggest claim to fame was that Brenda Fassie had once bought a pack of cigarettes there when she drove through Kasi. I hadn't seen her and neither had my parents—it was apparently on a day when Papa had been buying stock in town—but Basi swears that it's true, so it must be.

The big sign, painted with red against a white background, said: *Tshwene's General Store*. Tshwene being my father's family totem animal, of course, as well as his first name; also our grandfather's name and my brother's middle name. Everyone called the shop *ko* Tshwene, and before there was any other option for buying groceries, just *shoppong*.

As we drove in that day the usual group of young men were loitering on the front stoep, calling over every girl who walked by and hissing at the ones who ignored them. I had seen them make girls cry. They would curse a girl, or reveal some deeply personal and shaming gossip about her, and she would burst into tears as soon as she was out of their sight.

The shop was also a place where lovers met. When a girl and her lover could not meet anywhere else, they could be seen around the corner of the building kissing or talking with their arms around each other. The shop was where you heard things about people that you were not supposed to, where girls could be in love away from the disapproving eyes of their parents, and where boys could show off their girls. Ole had even told me that she had seen some people do a lot more than kiss and hold hands behind the shop, on the days when my father was not there.

"Steamy windows," she had said, making us both giggle.

I was very curious about that. When my father was not there, I spent much of my time at the shop making excuses to go out to the back, hoping to catch a glimpse of a couple in a car with steamy windows. Aus' Johanna had finally said, "They won't do anything when you're here."

"But Papa's not here. Mama's not here," I'd pointed out.

"No, but you are. They're not afraid of Basi, but they think you'll tell your parents."

"Me?" I was offended.

"Yes," she said, raising one eyebrow and looking straight into my eyes. "You. You talk."

To console me, Basi later explained that it wasn't that they feared I would run to tell my parents. It was that everyone saw me as being so afraid of my parents that if either one of them asked, I would be honest.

"I don't tell on you," I'd protested.

"No," he'd laughed. "But I'm your brother. That's different."

So I never saw anything.

As we walked in that day, a young man who was about two years older than Basi, a fat boy called Five Bop, because he was always penniless and asking friends for five bop to buy something, was calling over a girl with a short denim skirt, a red blouse, and short heels. "*Ee*, baby! I just want to hold your hand!"

The girl said something I didn't hear, but which was clearly hostile because Five Bop retorted, "*Haai*, man! You're not even pretty. I was doing you a favour. *Mxm!*"

Mama said, light-heartedly, "Five Bop, wash my car and have a job. Leave the girls alone."

Five Bop stood at attention, took off his hat and smiled politely at my mother.

"*Eeng*, Aus' Dimpho, I'll wash it," he said.

Sometimes our parents paid Five Bop and other loitering young men to do odd jobs around the shop, like carrying in boxes of stock, fixing a faulty fridge, taking out the rubbish, or cleaning around the place.

"Heita, Five," Basi said with his easy laugh and went to shake his hand. As soon as Mama had walked through the door, Five Bop pulled Basi over and whispered in his ear, but not so softly that I didn't hear.

"Give me a cigarette, 'fana," he said.

Basi smiled broadly and said, "Sure, Five. Sure, sure," and then he strolled inside and back out again, handing Five Bop a cigarette concealed under a handshake.

In the shop, the workers smiled and greeted us cheerfully. Aus' Johanna behind the counter waved at me, four of her right-hand fingers adorned with slim gold rings. Her hair always looked perfect: silky and shiny and brushed back. She wore a black-and-white dress—the colours Mama required the workers to wear so that, she said, they looked neat and tidy. Mama had also read somewhere that it builds teamwork to have workers wear a uniform. Papa had refused, so they had agreed on everyone wearing their own clothes, but in just those two colours.

Behind her and to the right, Bra Sticks stood at the second till and yelled out, "*Eeeh! Bana!*" when he saw us. He was a tall, skinny man who was endlessly cheerful and greeted us the same way every day.

Basi and I, as always, went right to work while someone made us something to eat. Basi sat behind the till and I stood behind the front counter and waited to serve people. I pulled whatever item the customer asked for from the shelves behind me and handed them over to the person before they went to Basi to pay at the till. Aus' Johanna, as always, started with the gossip as we worked. When Aus' Johanna was not on duty, it was Aus' Dolly—so-called because she had very light skin and very fine hair. She was also as quiet as a doll, so I preferred Aus' Johanna.

I remember feeling light and happy that day, watching Basi

tell Papa at the till about the rugby, and seeing Papa laugh, clap his hands, and pat Basi affectionately on the back. Craven Week, then SA Schools, quite possibly. I laughed as I watched. "*Heh!*" Papa yelled uncharacteristically at everyone. "Listen to this—" he was starting to say, but Basi stopped him with a bit of embarrassment.

"Papa, wait two weeks."

"Ho-right," Papa conceded. "Ho-right, ho-right."

Shoppers and workers who had stopped to listen went back to their work.

"*Ke eng?*" Aus' Johanna asked me, eyes wide open while she held a box of snuff in her hand and kept a customer waiting.

"Rugby," I said.

"*Rugby?*" She waved me away. "Oh-ho." She put the snuff in front of the customer. Nothing could make her care about rugby. "Why don't you play soccer at your schools?"

She tended to say "your schools" with such scorn that it made me laugh with embarrassment.

A little while later, Basi and I sat eating in the kitchen at the back while someone took over our work.

"Why didn't you want Papa to tell people?" I said in English.

"Two weeks," he said, in between bites. "I don't want anyone announcing it before it happens."

He was speaking Setswana—Basi hardly spoke a word of English when we were in Kasi. It was a matter of principle for him and he always winced with shame whenever I did. At home it was fine, but not down there. Never in front of other people. He was downright apologetic about going to the kinds of schools that we went to. And if it had ever been in him to be so impolite, then he would have told me to stop. He only switched languages and hoped that I would too, which I did.

But then he moved his chair closer and looked about to make sure no one was within earshot.

"I'm leaving early today," he told me. "Tell Papa I had to go see Kgosi. He's hurt himself in a soccer match at school."

"He has?" I raised my hand to cover the sight of the delicious pap and vleis in my mouth.

"No. But just say that." He seemed very anxious and hurried, constantly glancing up at the kitchen clock on the wall behind me.

I was annoyed. I liked talking to him about the goings-on at the shop. Plus, neither of us ever left the shop before the end of the day unless we had a lot of homework. Basi tended to do his homework in one sitting and not bother doing it bit by bit through the week. So really, if anyone ever left early, it tended to be me.

"Are you going to see that girl?" I whispered in irritation.

He raised his eyebrows at my tone.

"Moipone," I said in an even lower whisper.

Basi gave me a distant smile as if he were already gone. "Just say that. OK?"

I nodded.

He looked down thoughtfully at his clothes, and then seemed to get himself sorted as he stood up and put away his plate, wiping his mouth with a serviette before throwing it in the rubbish.

"Five!" he yelled at Five Bop, who was putting away car-wash cloths at the opposite end of the shop. "Did you tell Kgosi I was coming to see him?"

"Sure, jo," Five said without missing a beat.

"Ma!" Basi yelled to our mother, who was in the office sorting out papers. "I'll be back soon. I have to see Kgosi—he's hurt."

Five Bop added, "It's bad, jo. It's bad."

Before she could move from behind the desk, Basi was waving goodbye.

"I'll be back before we close!" he yelled and hurried out, with Five Bop taking his place at the till.

Mama looked in disbelief from the door to the till and then turned to Papa, who was stacking groceries onto the back shelves. He dismissed her concerns with an easy laugh. For some reason he was quite fond of Kgosi. He had once told my mother, "Nothing holds a man together like a childhood friendship. Let them be."

Unlike him, I was stunned—and quite irritated. Basi and Five Bop had worked together as if it had all been a simple part of their day: say hello, give cigarette, take over the till. I knew enough to realize that it hadn't been planned, that most things never were, that Basi and a lot of young men in Kasi spoke a secret men's language that required no translation. If Basi needed something and he wanted to make up an excuse, of course someone like Five Bop would understand, without even an explanation. Five Bop didn't need to know why—he just knew he had to help.

That was OK, normally. It was just that this time I knew that what Basi really wanted was to go and see Moipone, and he hadn't wanted to tell me the truth either. I had not been the one to cover for him. He had sold me almost the same story he had sold our parents. I realized then, as I had started to when I first met her, that Moipone was very much unlike any of the other girls Basi had gone out with—and that for reasons I found hard to grasp, I didn't like this fact at all. What's still curious is that to this day I haven't got a clue why he never talked about her with me.

Although I had been thinking obsessively about him, Kitsano was not the person on my mind when the phone rang that Monday evening.

Unlike a lot of boys, he had not waited too many days before he phoned for the first time. Even more surprising since he was older and in Standard Nine, and more reserved than most boys at his age.

Before Mama called my name at the top of her voice, I had been lying back in the bath, my feet resting at the far end. Once in a while when it got too cold I turned the hot water on with my toes. I liked the room very steamy so I always made sure the windows and the door were tightly shut when I filled up the bath.

"Save water," Mama used to say. "In Ethiopia people are struggling for enough water and you're wasting it."

"Two minutes from here people don't have water," Papa would say.

Once in a while I would get up to wipe the steam off the mirror that was across the room. Of course, every time I did this I would tread water across the floor, making the cream bath mat (which matched all the cream bath towels) wetter and wetter, so that by the time I was finished my bath the floor was slippery and the bath mat soaked, which quite annoyed Mama. It was just as I was putting my feet back in after one of these trips that I heard the phone ring.

Although I had been hoping it would be Kitsano every time, this time I had been in the middle of wondering about Basi and the rather bizarre end to the day involving him and Kgosi.

Basi had stayed away for a really long time and not come back until the very last minute to help with the money counting and everything that had to be done before we closed the shop. Five Bop had dutifully stayed at the till and happily earned a small sum, leading me to understand also that Basi had probably factored in how much money Five Bop would earn at the till, and how grateful Five Bop would be if Basi inconveniently disappeared.

But why had Basi been gone for so long? And more importantly, what had happened to their faces—his and Kgosi's?

Of course he had been with Kgosi, who later—after all the questioning and Mama being all *deurmekaar* and running to the bathroom aisle of the shop to find Band-Aid—helped us close up by packing away some of the stock that Papa had not had a chance to get to. Neither one of them said much, in spite of the fact that Kgosi's clothes were dishevelled and his hair powdered with sand. Basi's eye was swollen and his shirt had what looked like a drop of blood on it. Yet neither of them looked out of sorts. Kgosi went straight to the back and started chatting cheerfully with Papa, helping him with the last bit of stacking the back shelves. He said something to Papa that I couldn't hear from where I was standing, stunned, and they both roared with laughter. Papa even patted him proudly on the back.

Basi gave me a smile and a wink with the eye that was not purple and swollen, and proceeded to go to the office to help Mama count the money. I just stood dumbfounded and stared.

"Basi! Basi! *Dula, dula!*" Mama was saying.

He must not have bothered to obey, because eventually I heard the screech of a chair being dragged across the floor. That was when I finally managed to move from my position and run after him to the office, knocking over a box of tampons from the bathroom aisle and thinking how much more embarrassing that would have been if Papa, Kgosi, or Basi had seen it. I flew into the office to see Basi standing behind the desk, composed as ever, counting the last of the bank notes, which Mama would take to the bank early the next morning. He smiled easily at me and continued to count.

"What happened?" I tried to steady my voice but was unsuccessful because I was out of breath.

Mama held on to the back of the chair that she had only a few moments before dragged over for him to sit on.

"Basi?" She was as agitated as ever. "Who was it? Tell me. Who was it?" She put her hand on her mouth and then dropped it. And then: "How many times have I told you to stop—" but I cut her off.

"Did you have an accident?" I asked.

"No," he said, without looking up at either one of us.

Mama and I looked at each other curiously.

Basi put an elastic band around the ten-rand notes he had been counting and slowly put them beside the rest of the money. Then he picked up a bunch of fifties, licked his thumb and started counting. Then he paused.

"Look," he said in English, and continued counting as he spoke, "it was nothing to worry about. Some guys just said some things, and Kgosi and I got excited. It's all sorted out and we're both fine."

Mama sat down on the chair and took a deep breath. With much drama, she put both hands on the desk, and spread her arms across and gripped the edges. She bowed her head and whispered with much gravity, "Basimane. I have told you to stay away from down there. I have told you many times—many times!—to stay away . . . away from that boy!" She lifted her head and pointed towards the office door.

I immediately closed it and hoped that Kgosi hadn't heard.

Basi stopped counting. He put down the money and folded his arms, looking straight down at the notes, and took a deep breath through his nose.

He took another deep breath and then another.

No one moved. You could have heard a snake's hiss all the way in the Kalahari. Then he closed his eyes for what seemed like a long time. When he picked up the money he counted it so quickly and furiously that I was worried he was actually going to throw something. But he didn't. We both watched him, holding our breaths until he was finished. He took the bank bags, filled them, fastened the drawstrings and walked out of the office.

"Five!" we heard him call out. "Let's take Chief home." Most people called Kgosi by the English translation of his name.

Before we could say anything, we heard the car rev up outside and the boys were gone.

"What happened? Did Kgosi tell you?" Mama asked Papa later as the three of us set off for home in Mama's car. Basi and Five Bop had given Kgosi a lift home in Papa's car, as they sometimes did with the other employees—that being Papa's work-and-errands car, and not his personal, fancier one, which he left at home.

"Ah, boys," he said, steering the wheel to turn towards our gate. "Girl business. What else?" He laughed—heartily and alone—leaving my mother and me with our own private turmoil.

I was thinking then, as I got back into the bath, that if Basi had claimed when he left that Kgosi was not well, the fact that Kgosi had seemed perfectly fine later on hadn't bothered anyone. I wondered also how long Basi had been going out with Moipone, and how long it had taken him to bring her over to our house and introduce her to me. The only person to ask would be Kgosi—but he would also be the last person to tell.

So my mind was a bit muddled when Mama opened the door and stretched her hand, with the phone in it, towards me. I stood up to reach it but she pulled it back before I could, her eyes surveying the wet floor. I wrapped myself up with my bare arms and wished she hadn't let in the draught.

"You'll have to wipe that floor before you leave this bathroom," she said in a loud whisper.

I glared at her, but that was a bad idea because she took the phone back and put her hands on her hips. Not quite knowing what to do, I sat down in the bath and looked at her with what I hoped were apologetic and pleading eyes. She squinted at me, deciding on her course of action. It was all taking a long time and whoever was on the other end of the line was probably getting impatient, if they were still there.

"It's a boy," she finally said, accusingly.

My heart nearly jumped out of my chest.

"*Who* is it?" she asked.

I thought back to the social, and I thought it was best to keep quiet. So I shrugged. She handed me the phone and walked away, leaving the door open.

"Sorry," came the soft and excitingly deep voice from the other end. "Was it not a good time to call?"

"Ummm . . . no! No, it's . . . it's fine. Really. Uh . . . "

"Hi," he said with a little laugh.

"Hi," I said, trying to compose myself.

There was a long pause. I was trying to think of what Limakatso might say right at that moment. *Don't sound silly but don't seem like you're trying too hard,* I kept thinking. *I'm breathing too fast, my knees are too wobbly. I need to stop fidgeting. I've been quiet for too long—he'll think I'm a spaz.*

I cleared my throat. "Um, sorry. Hi. How are you?" *That's normal enough, I thought, but it doesn't sound very interesting. I'm not interesting. He'll be bored already.*

At the time he seemed a lot more at ease than I felt. He said, "I'm all right, you? I'm sorry. I guess you must be a bit . . . well, I should say why I called, shouldn't I?"

In retrospect I think he must have not been all that relaxed.

"No!" I pretty much screamed. *Gosh, Naledi, you sound so stupid.* I bit my lip and slapped my forehead. I felt my heart sink. I was completely lost.

Kitsano let out a soft laugh and said, "OK, well. Actually—"
But there was Mama at the door, tapping her finger on her wristwatch and holding up her hand with her pinky out and her thumb pressing her ear. I held up one finger and nodded furiously.

"Sorry. I think my mom wants the phone," I said.

"Wait!" he said, raising his voice for the first time. "I'm one of the Standard Nines who get to go to the matric dance this year—"

"Na-le-di!" Mama shouted.

"Oh," I started, walking to the door and mouthing, "Sorry, one minute," to her.

She clicked her tongue. I went back to sit anxiously on the bed.

By the time he said, "Do you want to be my date?" my fingernails had almost dug through the pillowcase.

"Um . . . I'll think about it," was what I said, because that was what Limakatso had told me you were supposed to say when boys asked you out. Even if you just wanted to scream, "Yes! Of course! I'd love to!"

"Oh, OK." He sounded surprised.

"OK . . . I mean . . . yes. I'll come. Thank you . . . I think . . . you know . . . I mean . . . yes. Thank you."

"Thank you . . . "

"For asking, I mean."

"Oh! I think, you know . . . thank you, really. For agreeing to come. I'm relieved. I won't have to wait by the phone."

"For what?"

"You know, for you to call."

Confused pause.

"You know . . . because you were saying you'd think about it."

"Oh! Oh, I mean . . . " We both laughed nervously. I took a deep breath. "I'm really excited," I admitted.

He said, "Me too," and I immediately wondered if that was the most desperate thing I could have said. I didn't know.

I've never felt sorrier to have to drop the phone. I wanted to phone both Limakatso and Kelelo straight away, to go over the conversation and the notes I had in my head. What had I done right, what had I done wrong and what should I have added? But I knew it would be too much to ask Mama after being on the phone for so long.

With a boy.

8

IT WAS EXACTLY TWO DAYS later that Mama came in, looking as harried as I had ever seen her. I know it was two days later because that was how long I took before picking up the phone and phoning Kitsano back. Limakatso and Kelelo had had two very serious discussions with me about how to behave at this juncture.

"OK," Limakatso had said as she nibbled on a carrot because she was on a diet, "don't look desperate."

We were sitting in our usual place on the grass, legs crossed, our lunch boxes in front of us.

"Sound like you have other offers," she said.

"*Say* you have other offers," Kelelo said opening her Tab—because she was watching her weight too.

"No! No, no, no! Don't say that." Limakatso was firm. "Just *make him think* someone else wants you to go."

I looked down at the egg-mayo sandwich that I had hurriedly prepared that morning and wondered if it was fattening and if maybe now was the time to lose some weight. As if they were reading my thoughts, Limakatso took the sandwich and examined it and Kelelo said, "Mayonnaise is very fattening."

I took a sip of her Tab and eyed Limakatso's lunch box, wondering if I would manage to not feel hungry on just carrots. She handed them to me before I asked.

"So what *exactly* did he say?" Limakatso was always really bossy about what to do with boys, which Kelelo and I liked and respected because she was six months older than both of us and had experience.

"OK. He said, 'Do you want to be my date?'"

"Just like that?" asked Kelelo.

"Just like that."

"And he sounded sure of himself? Really confident?" Limakatso now had her elbows resting on her thighs and her hands intensely clasped together, both forefingers pushing up against her chin.

Kelelo and I laughed.

"Hey, you guys! Boy business is serious business."

"Yes." I nodded emphatically in my mock-serious voice. "He sounded confident."

"Then he's dead serious, and from what I've heard—and I'm hearing a lot—he doesn't play around. So. Two days is what you give him."

"Two days?"

"Two days. One just to make him wait longer and two just to say, 'I'm not desperate.'"

"Two days. OK. Yes, ma'am."

Limakatso rolled her eyes with a faint smile.

Then I grinned anxiously and said, "You guys, I actually already said yes."

"Oh my gosh!"

"Naledi!"

I had been imagining that Kitsano might change his mind. Maybe he had been thinking of another girl to ask if I said no. *If anyone has had other offers, it would surely be him*, I was thinking. I knew that there were a lot of girls in Pretoria who really wanted to go out with him. Limakatso had found out from what she called her "inquiries" that I was, as she put it, "lucky" to have had him ask me out. I never admitted this to my friends but I had secretly wondered if it had anything to do with his obvious admiration for Basi. Of course, I didn't like to think of it that way.

So it was later on when I was home—and about to phone Limakatso just to go over what she really thought of me saying yes immediately—when Mama interrupted. I think that I had probably only dialled the first two numbers when I heard her yelling from the sitting room, "Ba-si-ma-ne!" and I put the phone down knowing that whatever it was, it was bad. Mama hardly ever called Basi by his full name. She said "Basi," or "*ngwanake*," or sometimes when we were around, say, our aunts or some of the other parents at Basi's school, she would say "son" in English. "Basimane" was reserved for only the most egregious offenses.

I put my finger on the receiver's drop button and listened from the passage, a few steps from the sitting room but well within earshot if I kept quiet and they didn't close the door.

In the kitchen Aus' Tselane stopped washing the dishes and I could see her wipe her hands on her apron as she made a swift exit, quietly closing the door behind her. She was probably going to her room. Aus' Tselane was the quietest, most polite of all the helpers we had ever had. I remember a stout woman called Mme Maria, who had been with us a few years before that, just before I started high school, who would sit with me for an hour when I came home from school and tell me all kinds of things about her family and the families of the people who worked at the shop, because many of them were her neighbours. I had loved her, with her colourful scarves that she sometimes wrapped around her head and sometimes around her waist. She was a tall, stout, and opinionated woman who Mama had said talked too much. Mama would say that in English in front of her, because she didn't speak a word of English. She made me the sweetest, most delicious tea and we would drink it in the kitchen in the fading light of the afternoon sun. She was with us for quite a while. I loved having her around, but she had been transferred to the shop because Mama found her "too much." Aus' Tselane was fine, but I wished she would talk more. I never knew what was on her mind—like on this particular evening.

She liked to leave people to their business—which I suppose is all right. It's a trait I've never had. So, naturally when she walked out, I moved a few steps closer, sliding over the tiled floor in my school socks—the tiles were a light beige colour that the shop had called gold, but they never quite looked golden to me.

"Never, never! You must never . . . " Mama was saying.

The front door slammed shut and I knew that Papa had come in.

"Basimane, our son," she said but then stopped and I could hear her loud and desperate breathing.

I wished that I could see Basi then: where he was sitting; the look on his face. What had he done?

"I know, I know," I heard Papa say. "Let's all sit down. Sit down, Basimane."

Oh, I wished I could be in the same room! My chest hurt from the heavy drumbeat of my heart. I wanted to go in and sit down too, but had to stay as quiet as a prowling cheetah near an impala. They could all go quiet and then I would end up not having heard anything.

"You knew?" Mama said to Papa.

He must have nodded because I heard the furious chiming of her bangles and then the *thwat!* of her hands coming down against her thighs.

"It was one visit," Papa said.

Basi still had not said anything, hadn't defended himself.

I heard Mama's voice rise—"One!"—and then fall in a furious, low growl. "*One?!*"

"Dimpho." Papa spoke in an even, measured voice. "I think

once in a while it's OK to help a friend. Kgosi couldn't have gone alone, could he?"

"Let him go alone!" Mama screeched.

"Never." Basi's voice finally spoke out in his own defence—or Kgosi's? "Never," he repeated, his voice louder than usual but as clear and determined as ever.

More than the anger you could hear the fight in it. I knew—I had always known, hadn't I?—that you don't fight Basi over Kgosi. Two male lions in the wild? You don't go near them if you know what's good for you.

A cold, long silence fell over the sitting room—over the whole house—and I don't know how long this would have gone on had Kitsano not phoned me himself at that very inopportune moment.

Although I'm not complaining, because when he said, "Are you OK?" I almost forgot what I had been doing.

"I'm OK. Family drama." I tried to sound nonchalant but I think my voice was shaking both from what I had just heard and from hearing his voice.

"I just wanted to tell you that I'm looking forward to the dance."

He was so polite, Kitsano; unlike a lot of boys I knew. Sometimes I thought that maybe he spoke English only after directly translating it from Setswana in his head. Most boys would have said, "OK, cool. I'll see you." But he said, "I'm looking forward to it." And then: "I'll have the most beautiful date." My back tingled from that.

The most beautiful date . . .

Just then Basi marched furiously out of the sitting room and slammed the door to his bedroom. Slammed it!

Basi didn't slam things—or hadn't until then.

9

"HOW DO YOU KNOW when you're in love?" I asked Ole when she came to our house the following Saturday morning. It was only three weekends before what would be Basi's last weekend at home. Although none of us knew it then, did we?

Ole sat at the edge of the bath with her feet (in faded brown boots) stretched out in front of her. She was constantly adjusting her Dobbs hat. I glanced at her and realized that her hands always needed to be busy with something. She was always either smoking or adjusting her hat.

By the time she answered my question that realization had brought on another question: Was it possible that she was always nervous? I fidgeted a lot, and everyone knew I lacked composure. It wasn't something that had occurred to me about Ole.

She said, "You act like a stupid person," which might have stung had I not known her better. But I only felt a bit disoriented.

"I do?" I was standing at the sink facing the mirror with my gloves on, smearing more of my white relaxer cream into my hair. I turned around to look at her when I said that, blinking because my eyes stung from the cream.

She folded her arms rather tightly and lifted her shoulders, as if she were cold.

"That's how you know. You know you're in love when you act like a stupid person."

I laughed and mixed in the rest of the relaxer. After I had put away the gloves I opened the bathroom window to let in some air. She took out a cigarette from her jacket pocket—a smart-looking men's jacket—and pointed it towards me with a questioning look. I nodded and she led the way into my bedroom. My parents would not be home for a long time so it was OK to smoke.

In my room she stood leaning out the high window, her elbows perched on the windowsill and the cigarette in her left hand. Occasionally she would make a show of fanning the smoke. I watched her from where I was sitting at the edge of my bed and thought about something I wanted to ask her. I clutched at my red teddy bear, which Basi had bought me the year that I was ten and he was fourteen, when he had received a box full of Valentine's Day cards and I had received two from Limakatso and Kelelo. He had bought me this teddy bear holding a big heart that said "i love you," just to make me feel special.

I was nervous about asking Ole the question, since we never really talked about her and boys. Not really—not unless it was a joke. Casually, although I didn't feel so casual, I said, "You've never been in love?" and then was immediately afraid I had taken it too far. From a distance I thought that I could see her body stiffen. I gripped the bear tightly around its feet and held it close and it seemed as if nothing moved for a very long moment.

She turned around and glanced at me and then she looked back out of the window and took a long drag on the cigarette. I cleared my throat. "Because . . . then how would you know?"

"How would you know what people feel when they're in love?" Her voice was barely above a whisper but she didn't look back at me. She just kept smoking and then tossed the cigarette out into our garden.

She had to be nervous because she would never otherwise have done that. My mother would kill someone if she found something so disgusting on her lawn.

Ole turned around to look at me. She rested her back against the wall and folded her arms around her. Her eyes looked at mine only briefly before they moved on to my dressing table.

"Deepest, darkest secret?" Her eyes darted briefly from the table to me and then back. She gave a short, forced laugh, like she had just made a failed attempt at a joke.

I didn't say anything, knowing that if I said something wrong, she wouldn't tell me anything.

"I've been in love," she said without bringing her eyes back to me. "For sure."

"For sure?" I was suddenly feeling rather bold and had to hold on to the teddy to stop myself from asking all the questions in my head.

"Not for sure like we say *ko* Kasi, like it means maybe." She cleared her throat again and looked down at her shoes. "Ja. I've been in love."

"With whom?"

She rubbed her face as if she were tired. She readjusted her hat, pulling it down so that it almost covered her eyes, and then shoved both hands into the pockets of her baggy pants while she stared at her shoes. Then she nodded slowly to herself before forcing a grin.

"Someone. A beautiful person." She rolled her eyes as if she were mocking someone.

"Who?"

Ole threw her hands in the air with a dramatic sigh.

"Aaaggg . . . ! A girl! All right? A chick. *Ngwanyana*. Cherrie. *Umfazi*, or whatever you want to call her. A chick." She walked over to my side and threw herself on my bed, where she lay on her back and pushed her hat forward so that it completely covered her face.

I felt . . . awkward, yes, but a lot less uncomfortable than I would have imagined I would feel. There had been rumours. When we lived in Kasi people were always saying, "Ole *ke sempatle mo banyaneng.*" That's what they would say about girls who preferred the friendship of boys: "She's a don't-look-for-me-in-the-company-of-girls." The opposite if it were a boy. They'd shorten it to "*sempatle.*" It was quite simple and meant no harm—at least not to me, who was never called that.

This, this moment when Ole said it to me, watching her expression and seeing how exposed she probably felt, this made me wonder how I would have felt. Of course I didn't know what to say, but being the fidgety person I am, I tried to make it all less awkward. Deepest, darkest secret indeed.

"Can you tell me her name?" I tried to sound upbeat.

I was rewarded when I saw the look of relief mixed with confusion on her face.

"What? Most people would say, 'You're gay?' Not 'What's her name?'" She sat up and smiled at me. But looking suddenly serious again, she added, "That's what people have said, anyway."

My minor triumph was replaced with a tinge of jealousy. "You've told other people?"

"Just Miss Natalia, the guidance counsellor. She's great," she said.

"You could have told me, you know. I'm . . . I'm great! We're like . . . like sisters or something."

Ole moved closer to me and looked me straight in the eye. This time she sat up straight and clasped both hands in front of her.

"You *love* boys." She spat it out like an accusation.

"So?" I was offended but didn't really know why. I felt the same as when I was told that people only trusted Basi not to tell our parents what they did at the back of the shop. People didn't know me that well, I wanted to say. But at the same time I couldn't vehemently launch a convincing defence.

"You and your friends, Limakatso and Kelelo. Why do you think I've never come to sit with you when our schools meet for games? We see each other at galas and matches. Why do we only hang out at home?"

"I don't know. You're always reading—"

"Studying? Yes, all the time. I'm on a bursary, I have to pass."

"*And*," I sidestepped the money comment, "anyway, at school . . . with my friends . . . we only talk about boys a little bit," I countered weakly.

Ole raised a questioning eyebrow. It was my turn to throw my hands in the air.

"OK!" I yelled. Then less audibly: "I have a thing for boys."

We both laughed.

"And I thought you wouldn't understand," she said.

I was about to add imprudently that it was not entirely a secret, her romantic interest in girls. But my scalp was burning and I had to run to the bathroom to rinse out the relaxer. After I had shampooed it and was waiting for the conditioner to work I sat at my dressing table with my back to Ole, who was on to her second cigarette.

"I think I'm in love. Anyway. I think."

She turned to me and said, "That's nice," without a hint of sarcasm.

"I think my brother's also in love," I added, turning to face her.

Here she turned her back to me and took a drag of the cigarette. When she blew out the smoke she said, kind of slowly, "With . . . Moipone?"

"I think so," I said.

There was a long, silent moment before she said, "He's not her type."

I didn't know what she meant, so I said, "But they're going out. She's going out with him."

Ole sighed and then, looking at the floor, she said in a sing-song voice, "Then I hope he doesn't mess it up."

"I think he *really* likes her," I added with emphasis.

Ole held her left hand with the cigarette out of the window and rested her right hand on the wall at face level, then turned to face me. Her tone was more than matter-of-fact. It had a hint of anger.

"Your brother likes a *lot* of things."

"What does that mean?" I said indignantly, not able to look her in the eye. I suddenly had the urge to slap her and it was so unlike anything that I had ever felt towards her that it shook me a bit.

"Nothing. I hope they're happy."

I stared at her back for a long time, just watching her smoke. When she didn't turn around, I walked out to go and rinse my hair.

10

IT WAS ONLY THE NEXT DAY that I had a chance to speak to Basi about Moipone. Those days, finding him felt like chasing a rabbit in the woods. If you blinked you would miss him.

Now, it had never been disputed that my brother was a very good-looking young man. Sometimes, when he passed a glass door or caught a glimpse of himself in a mirror, his eyes would go up and down, taking in his full frame. His eyebrows would rise in a flash of surprise, as if he couldn't quite believe the perfection himself. But then he would compose himself in that very quick, skilled way that he seemed to have trained himself in, and if you hadn't been looking carefully from the start you would have missed it. I never missed it.

"He got my good looks," Mama liked to say, looking in wonder at her boy.

I envied the good looks. So I watched him too, sometimes in awe.

There were the high cheekbones that are the family trademark, the long nose that he got from my father and not the short, small one that I got from my mother. (She disagrees.) There are the full, darker-than-his-face lips and the slightly sticking-out ears that girls at my school told me was a big part of his charm.

I watched him from the doorway of his room that Sunday morning. He looked like someone getting ready for a big event—smoothing an eyebrow, pulling at the shirt, flicking fluff off his jeans—and the strangest thing struck me. He didn't seem so sure of himself. There was no delight at his own image. Instead I thought: *He actually looks unsure.* My shoulders drooped involuntarily.

"What is it?" I asked. I must have sounded concerned because he quickly got hold of his senses and, well, *feigned* contentment. And then, as he usually did, Basi fell into a sort of ease with himself, the way he could do in an instant, like a soldier commanding himself to stand at attention. He turned to me and that easy smile came and lit up his face.

"Heeey, Nedi, my Nedi," he said, rubbing his hands together like he was getting ready to work with them. "Howzit?"

"Basi," I said, "you have to go to the shop today. Papa—"

He waved away my concern. "I'll be at the shop. Just a little later." He was talking to his reflection. "I just have to go and do something *ko* Kasi, OK? I'll be there."

"Papa said . . . " I started, emphatic. "He said he wants us both there for the tills today when the staff go home early for Sunday lunch. He needs some help."

Basi seemed not to have heard. I waited, watched him turn for a moment to scan the room with his eyes and then turn back to the mirror for one last look.

"Basi?" I walked in and lay on the bed, on my stomach.

"*Heh?*"

"Moipone's very pretty."

He turned to me quickly, threw the brush on the bed and put his hands in his pockets. His grin was wide and satisfied.

"I know! I know. She's . . . " I thought he would say "a beaut," but his mind seemed to drift off and his face took on a more serious look.

"She's what?" I didn't know why my heart was racing.

"She's . . . *something*," he said, pensive and nodding slowly. "She's really something." Then he was looking around the room again, eyes searching. Finally, he located his cologne, a bottle of strong-smelling liquid our aunt Lele had bought him the year before for his birthday. Which he had never used. He and I had once joked about it, saying that it made him smell like the ocean. Which was the point, since it was called The Beach.

I pulled at my tiny ponytail. "You're wearing that?"

But he barely heard me. He sprayed it on his hands and then smeared it on his neck, something we had seen Papa doing many times. Basi smelled it, and then held up the mostly full bottle and examined it. The scent was overwhelming. But he wasn't convinced. He lifted his shirt and sprayed a little more underneath it. The mist sprayed upwards, hit his chin and went directly into his nose.

We both coughed and I waved my hand in the cloudy air.

"What *are* you doing?!" I coughed some more, just to make the point, while he moved to open the window.

"Too much?" he said, the bottle still in his hand, forefinger threatening to press.

"Uh . . . yes. Yes, I think definitely too much." I reached over and slowly took it from him, exaggerating my movements as if I were taking a gun from a madman—which sent us into a fit of laughter.

"OK, Basi," I started, putting the bottle down. "You haven't been at the shop as much as you're supposed—"

"I know." He spoke softly, reassuringly, with both hands on my shoulders. "I'll be there." There was that no-worries grin again.

"If I get there before you—"

"Nedi, relax."

I put up both hands to indicate that I was letting that go. Then I went and sat on his bed.

"OK, now . . . What was Mama angry about last week?" I

thought that he would stiffen up and make excuses but instead he laughed!

"Oh, that!" He brushed it off with a wave of the hand.

"Yes, that. She was so angry. What happened?"

He came to sit down next to me on the bed and shook his head.

"OK. I went to the jail and—"

"The jail?"

"Yes, the jail." He was serious and unmoved by my shock. "I went with Kgosi for a visit." He turned to face me, his right palm resting on the bed and his left palm on his thigh. He looked all pensive and businesslike when he assumed this posture. "Mama was upset about the jail and then she was upset about the fight last week."

"When you came into the store with cuts and bruises?" I said, pointing an accusing finger. "And you wouldn't say—"

"Yes, yes." He waved that away and sat with his head bent over.

"You've been there before, haven't you?" The words came out as the thought formed in my mind.

Basi nodded without looking at me.

"Man, Nedi. It's really rough. I mean, really, really hard over there." He stood up slowly and went to sit at his desk, facing me. There was anger in his voice. "It's not fair either, you know. It's so unfair." He furrowed his brow. "She shouldn't *be* in there. It was self-defence. It's always been self-defence. Those bastards, those . . . idiots!" He rolled his hands into fists and then bit his lips. "They don't know . . . *no one* knows what she's been through. And . . . you know . . . who are they? Who has the right to judge her, and put her in there?"

I recognized that this wasn't a question.

"Man, when I'm a lawyer . . . " His voice trailed off.

Basi said that a lot. It was a well-known family fact that Basi would study law at UCT, and defend "the common man." He always stated this with conviction.

Mama used to say, "Or a doctor. You could be whatever you want, really. You got my brains."

When people asked me what I wanted to be, I would say a writer, but never with the same amount of confidence. "Or a theatre director," I would sometimes add.

"You have enough stories," Mama would say with a laugh. "You'll do either one just fine."

Basi licked his lips and inhaled deeply through his nose.

"They have them in these cells . . . " He shook his head as if shaking away a memory. "Anyway," he said, sitting up straight again, "hopefully she'll be out soon."

I looked outside and saw the sun shining on the tin roof of the back rooms. It made me think of Silver City. The tree just outside Basi's room, the one he had sometimes climbed down when we first moved here, now had no apricots on it. Winter was nearly here.

What I had always heard about Kgosi's mother's case was that she had killed her husband—her very hard-working husband who had done a lot for the country as an MK fighter. Kgosi's mother was mad, people said. And these people included Mama. She said there had always been something wrong with her.

"I was never surprised that she married a man like that," she once told me. "She was always fighting. It's no wonder she married someone who was fighting all the time. If she could have, she probably would have gone off to the wild with him and carried a gun like the rest of them." She had always been a restless woman, according to Mama.

"Anyway, the fight was funny." This was Basi changing the subject and bringing me back to the room.

"What fight? What happened?"

"Just some guys said something to Kgosi, and I threw some

punches." He was hitting his fist on his chair and laughing. "There were two of them and three of us so—"

"Three?"

"Thibedi came and took them down with us." Thibedi was Five Bop's cousin and lived with Five's parents. Basi was demonstrating, throwing punches in the air and stomping his foot on the carpet. Finally he sat down, threw his head back and laughed so loudly that I could see the roof of his mouth.

"Aaaah," he said, lightly dabbing his still-bruised eye with his thumb. "Kgosi has done the same for me. Has some scars to show for it, too." His laughter died down and he rubbed his back with one hand, looking at his watch with the other.

My mind was back at Kgosi's mother.

"She shot him, right?" I had never asked outright. Basi didn't discuss Kgosi's family affairs. He always got angry when it came up, but he never quite shared his opinion on that.

He stood up.

"She did. And good for her, too. He would have killed her first if she hadn't. People don't know. Mama has no idea . . . the things I know . . . "

I knew the conversation was over. Every time Basi came close to revealing something that only he and Kgosi knew—and that he knew I was madly curious about—he'd stop himself just when I thought I was about to finally hear it. He brushed his eyebrows with his fingers, and turned and walked out of the room. Then, as if he had remembered something, he came back and stood in the doorway.

"Hey . . . so, you're coming to the dance at my school, I hear?"

My heart lifted. I had been thinking so much about him and Ole that my own exciting news seemed to have been pushed aside.

"Yes," I said. "Yes, indeed."

He gave me a very pleased grin.

"Cool. He's a nice bloke. Hey, it's only two weeks after my big match at the other school."

"All-White school hey?"

"Eish," he said. "All White."

I knew he got nervous sometimes about these matches. The racial slurs hurled at him made him uneasy and he did say the constant attacks—which had sometimes left him badly bruised and cut—scared him, but he was also "going for gold" for Craven Week. I saw him take a deep breath.

"It'll be a great way to celebrate together."

For some reason I wished that he hadn't said that. I shivered unexpectedly and rubbed my arms, trying to ignore the bad feeling I suddenly had.

"Are you taking Moipone?" I said in an attempt to focus.

He grinned. "Definitely."

When Papa phoned from the shop asking where we were and if I would be walking down with Basi, I said yes, even though it was a lie.

Considering the cologne and the mood Basi had been in, I didn't quite trust that he would stick to his word. I told Papa, "He'll be there really soon," and could almost feel him frown on the other end of the phone. I didn't like lying to Papa, but Basi and I understood that we lied for each other when it was necessary. We not only did this effortlessly but also with pride. We each had an invisible spear and shield in front of us, which we brought out whenever the other needed it. I thought of us as hunters in the wild: tuck your friend behind you, hold the shield, point the spear and talk down the lion. But these were easier, simpler times.

In the end I arrived at the shop about thirty minutes before Basi. When he did arrive, he marched right into the office and kept himself busy for five minutes until he was interrupted by Papa, who closed the door for a while, probably chiding Basi for being late. Again.

11

A FEW DAYS LATER Mama took us to town to buy smart outfits for the matric dance at Basi's school. It was only three days before the big match—the one where there would be selectors picking the best boys from the team. The match that would most definitely turn my brother into a national rugby player. His school would be playing at the other school, facing them on the field for the first time. Basi was an experienced player, quite obviously one of the big stars of his team.

Despite his recent absences, our house was buzzing with excitement for the coming two big events—first the match, and then the dance two weeks later. So the trip to town was full of laughs and funny old stories. Mama was in an especially good mood; she and Basi talked about his varsity plans for a while, a topic that had come up a lot recently.

I caught bits and pieces of the conversation, but mostly I watched the world go by and fantasized about the matric dance and Kitsano. He'd gone back to Botswana for two weeks for a family wedding, and he would be back just in time for the dance.

I watched as three women climbed off a small white bakkie and then proceeded to unload bright fruit from the cab. Oranges and naartjies were almost in season. Soon there would be mounds of bright oranges displayed all along the roads. The women would be on their mats, covered in heavy blankets, shielding themselves and their babies from the cold.

The light turned green and we were off, speeding past drying leaves and yellowing grass by the roadside.

"*Heh! E fedile* apartheid!" Mama said as we passed workers putting up a new road sign to change its name from Malan to Mandela. "*No more!* No more, no more, no more Malan!" she said vehemently and then burst into angry laughter. "I remember one day, everyone having to jump out of a taxi because," she pointed to the rail tracks to our left, "people were being chased and shot at by police for not having passes on the train. We all ran like frightened impalas into the roads. *Heh!* I didn't know where I was going. Cars just stopped, the taxi wouldn't move, and we were all told, '*Heh, bathong!* Run!' And off we went." Mama leaned forward and ducked her head, putting one hand up as if she were shielding herself against the bullets at that very moment. "*Iyo! Tshabang! Shianang!*" She re-enacted the scene, sending Basi and me into fits of laughter. Funny how Mama could sometimes make apartheid years seem like an adventure—when she and Papa got in the mood, my brother and I could fall off our seats laughing.

So we were laughing when she parked the car, and still laughing when we walked into the women's section of the department store, where Mama wanted to pick up a few things. Basi was walking in front of me and Mama was behind me.

A woman—a White woman—saw Basi coming towards her and clutched her bag to her chest, pulling her little girl away from the clothes she was looking at and holding her close. Basi stepped around and made a point of walking as far away from them as possible.

Mama clicked her tongue and gave the woman a dirty look. The woman pushed her little girl in the opposite direction. I turned around and watched as she hastened with her out of the shop.

I felt quite angry. I wanted to say something, but didn't know what. Basi held out his hand to me and walked me over to a different section of the shop, where there were home decorations and linens.

"We should have said something."

Basi looked around him, raised his shoulders and feigned a shiver. "The women's department always makes me uneasy." He gave an easy Basi laugh and rubbed my back.

"White people will never change if we don't . . . " I insisted.

He shrugged, smiling calmly at me. There were no signs of him being upset.

"Come on, Nedi. We're going to walk out and someone else will clutch their purse or lock their car door just at the sight of me. You can't get upset about it every time." He put his arm around me. "*Makhoa* will always be scared, man. Apartheid or no apartheid. How do you unlearn that?" He turned pensive. "It's that feeling," he said. "The feeling that they're in the wild. That Africa is the wild and they're hunters. We're the lions. Be afraid," he added but didn't laugh this time.

By the time Mama came to meet us she also seemed to have forgotten about it.

"Five White people asked me to get them their size. I counted this time." She held up her hand to show us. "Five! I said, 'I don't work here, my dear. I just buy.'" She made the money sign with her thumb and middle fingers, then laughed so hard at her own joke that she held on to her stomach and her body bent forward as she moved on ahead of us and out through the door.

We bought Basi a pair of black pants and a light green shirt, and spent a lot of time deciding if he should go with a black tie, a green tie, or no tie. He had led us to this shop, a new one, owned by a tall and stylish Black man. Called St Aubrey's, it was one of the first of its kind in town, selling very smart and stylish men's clothes. Basi knew some of the staff; I recognized one of them from his school. Basi chatted away as he picked and chose his clothes. It was very nearly the end of the day by the time I went over to another shop to buy something for myself. I bought a little black dress, with Mama constantly saying, "I don't know if it's too short, Naledi. Let me look at you again." I was quite happy with it. *Kitsano will be amazed*, I kept thinking. It wasn't short enough, to be honest.

So we were making jokes and all three of us laughing happily when we arrived at the first signs of Silver City. Basi and I had let Mama play her own music—Teddy Pendergrass—which we liked to tease her about from time to time.

Mama was snapping her fingers and moving her head to the music. Basi sang along, half-mockingly, to the raspy-voiced Teddy's "Love T.K.O." Along the road friends and neighbours were reconnecting after a long day. Inside the houses, I knew, supper would be cooking on stoves, women staying close enough to watch that nothing burned. The aromas of *bogobe, nama,* and *seshabo* wafted out through open windows that were letting in the last of the sun's heat. I looked over at Mama and knew that she was content. We had had a good day in town and she was happy knowing that we would look nice and smart when the dance came.

Wow. Just over two weeks, I thought. I couldn't see myself waiting patiently for the time to come.

There we were going along, laughing and singing and clapping until Mama said, just as we turned onto the main road, the one that separates *di*Ex from *ko motseng,* "Isn't that Ole?"

I never really knew why—maybe it's growing up surrounded by storytellers and seeing stories divided into chapters narrated by different people—but I see life in clips sometimes. It comes, in my mind, in a series of beginnings and endings that define the laughter and the tears, the dreading and the hoping. So I have often taken moments and put them safely in a packet, carrying them around and then opening them up and reliving them when I need to. And that day, in the car, with the three of us driving home together from town, is definitely one of the good times.

Life doesn't work like that, of course (and if it did, there wouldn't be this story), but if you can package some of it neatly like that, then why not? Because, inevitably, what follows a good time like this is not just more singing and more laughter. That day, the minute Mama said, "Isn't that Ole?" we were thrown off abruptly from our bliss.

Because Ole wasn't alone. She was with Moipone. It wasn't as if Ole was standing on a street corner idly chatting away with Moipone. Ole wasn't just having a cigarette with a couple of boys—although that would have been scandalous and reproachful enough for Mama.

She was smoking a cigarette in one hand, while her other arm rested comfortably around Moipone.

"Eish, eish," was what Basi said. "I'll get off here and I'll see you at home later."

This, of course, infuriated Mama.

"You want to go too?" she said scornfully, turning to me. "See your friend?"

There were about two seconds there when I couldn't understand her because my eyes were stinging and my head was pounding painfully. We had stopped at the side of the road. Basi turned around and looked at me with pleading eyes, sending me a sign that, for once, I couldn't understand. The only thing I could do was nod, even though I wasn't sure who I was nodding to.

Then Basi turned around and hurriedly climbed out of the car, and I followed blindly. He held my hand and we crossed the street while Mama sped off.

It is curious, looking back, that Basi pulled Moipone away so abruptly—not roughly, I must add. Just abruptly, and barely acknowledging Ole. Ole and Moipone hadn't been aware of us until we were right in front of them. They were absorbed in conversation and sharing a laugh.

The thing is, two girls with their arms around each other wasn't an unusual sight. I held hands and sat on my friends' laps all the time. Girls did that. But I knew from far away, from the second I had turned to see if it actually was Ole, I knew that this wasn't just like me putting my arm around Limakatso or Kelelo's waist.

Basi stepped in and pulled Moipone by the hand without saying anything. Moipone turned her head to Ole and said, "I'll see you," and then her steps followed Basi's. Ole looked startled, but knowing her as well as I did (or as well as I thought I did at the time), I could see she was working hard to look unperturbed. She shoved her hands in her pockets and watched them walk away.

When Basi had Moipone at a safe distance he seemed to be trying to coax her into conversation. He had his hands on each of her cheeks while she looked down at the ground. Then he raised Moipone's chin with one of his hands. She looked up at him only for a few seconds and then she turned away. Ole and I watched, although she still hadn't acknowledged that I was standing next to her.

I was not particularly surprised by this scene—it was a familiar song and dance between men and women in Kasi. I had seen it many times: the man standing very close to the woman while she kept moving away from him. People said the man had to work very hard for a woman's attention, and the more resistance he encountered, the more honourable the woman was thought to be. When I was in primary school, when we still lived *ko motseng*, I remember boys twisting my wrist until it was dry and red. It was all part of the games boys and girls played, I was told. I got used to it, and the more a boy twisted my wrist the more I thought he liked me. But Ole always said it was disgusting.

Very, very slowly, Ole turned her head to look at me. I saw her face change as she adopted a more cheerful look: I wasn't supposed to see what she was feeling.

"My brother really likes her," was all I could think to say.

Ole forced a smile and kicked a small stone with her scruffy boots.

"Hmmm."

"Look at the way he looks at her," I added, watching Basi put his arm around Moipone.

"Let's go," Ole said and pulled me away.

I turned to look again at Basi and there, in the middle of the street and in broad daylight, my brother was kissing his girl-friend. I chit-chatted away, willing Ole not to look back, and she didn't, thank goodness—but just as I gave a sigh of relief as we turned the corner, she said, "Your mother would lose her mind. Basimane kissing a girl in the middle of the street like that would just kill her." She pulled out a cigarette and lit it.

Only Ole called Basi by his full name. It always sounded formal and this time it held a hint of hostility. It wasn't how people normally said my brother's name. People said "Basiiiii," like it wasn't so much a word as a pretty song. There was that sound of praise and joy mixed with a touch of respect when my brother's name was said. The same went for my father's name. Come to think of it, it was true of most men, really. Even hooligans like Five Bop. Men and boys were to be adored, as a rule. But with Ole, it was as if she had missed the community meeting and hadn't been informed of this decision.

I tried not to take offense at the way she said "Basimane," like she was recalling the bitter taste of unripe fruit. I didn't know what was going on and didn't want to ask. OK, fine, to say I didn't *want* to know would be more honest.

"Where are you going?" she asked. "You haven't been down here in a long time."

"Yes, I have. I come every—"

"Without your parents. Walking. Without a car."

I didn't go down *ko motseng* very much, it was true. I spent my life moving from our house into the car, from the car to school in town, or from the car to the shop, from the shop to our house and so on. The girls who took taxis to school had learnt to get around without their parents' cars, and made fun of me sometimes. Ole was one of them. A lot of the time she just rolled her eyes at the whole thing.

"I came . . . to the shop," I said finally.

I followed her through the streets, the two of us slowly making our way there. Ole said hello to many people as we went along, most of them groups of young men standing around at street corners, listening to music or throwing dice and gambling. They raised their hands and voices, greeting her like she was one of them. "Eh, Ole! Heita, *jo*." They invited her to play the way they only did with other boys, the way they never would with me. In fact some of them said, "Who's that cherrie, Ole?" and "Come introduce us to that sweet cherrie, Ole!" My ears twinged when one said, "Hey, Ole, where do you find these nice cherries? I like the one you were with before too."

They whistled and complemented my "nice legs" and "sweet lips." Ole took it all in stride. I secretly felt glad that I was with her and not just another girl, and I was struck by how Ole's social standing seemed to have changed. When we were little there had been a fair bit of teasing, but now the boys seemed to waver between ignoring her, teasing her, and sometimes having a cigarette with her. What they never did was whistle and make comments about how pretty she was. I didn't want to remind her how painful it had been at times, how she had gotten into fights with the boys. I had always felt sorry for her when her mother said, "Olebogeng, if you acted like a girl you wouldn't come home with a blue eye." I wouldn't want to be reminded if I were her.

Instead, I pushed back the memories and waved to people whose faces I thought I recognized. I hadn't been down there, on foot, I realized, in probably two years! We walked past children playing games, people standing at their gates talking and shouting happily (or not) across their fences to neighbours and friends. Mothers were calling children to come home, or sending them to buy something from the shops.

I reminisced quietly about what my mother called our "past life." It really did feel like another world. I had been so removed. Half my life was in town now. Most of the time I spoke English—both my parents and the school insisted on it. Most people I was around—apart from at the shop—spoke English. Except for Ole and Basi, of course. They went to school and made it work, then came home, washed their hands of it. They both acted like town and English were more a part of my world than theirs. It was a wonder they weren't friends.

I was more my mother's child, although she wouldn't say so. I rarely missed *motse*. Although I missed the clusters of girls giggling together, sitting under large trees braiding each others' hair or drinking cooldrink and biscuits on blankets on their front lawns. You couldn't people-watch in *diEx*. The walls were too high and the streets were too quiet.

When we walked down Ole's street, one street away from where we used to live, I felt like I had been transported back in time. There was the smell of chips from the corner house with the spaza shop—Nellie's Tuck Shop—where we used to buy *sephatlho*, and where the boy thought I was pretty and gave me a little extra atchar. There was Nkele's Sizzling Designs, the hair salon two houses down that had started as a small business but had grown so much that the owner—Nkele, a very beautiful and well-groomed woman then in her twenties—had had to build back rooms. You could smell the burning hair and fragrant hair products from the street.

We walked carefully around a game of Fish so as not to step on the perfect drawing on the ground; the little girls playing it looked at us appreciatively.

Through someone's backyard I saw our old house, a big white house that had been renovated years ago, standing larger and higher than the houses around it. It had been the biggest house on the street when we lived there, but slowly people had extended their apartheid houses so that the street had started to look grander and fancier. Although here people didn't build walls for fences: it was considered rude and downright hostile. Up in *di*Ex, however, high walls only sent the message that you could afford privacy. Ole once said, "The rich have different needs and different rules from the rest of us"—something she would later repeat under very different and much more painful circumstances.

I know they do. I mean I know *we* do.

Ole pointed to a faded-orange house with its front windows facing the street. Its door was a very bright red and so was its stoep, which had been polished and shone brightly against the fading late afternoon sun. She pointed with her cigarette.

"That's Moipone's house."

It was quiet and it looked like no one was at home. I glanced around curiously, unsure of what I was hoping to see.

"She lives just with her mother. She works late."

I nodded and kept examining the house as if it would give

me some clues about Moipone. Finally I asked, "Is her mama pretty?"

Ole laughed at that.

"She's pretty. She's *very* pretty. She used to be Miss Marapong when she was in high school."

I could only imagine, given Moipone's looks.

"There she is." Ole pointed to a tall, slim woman with shoulder-length hair walking up the street towards us.

She wore a knee-length light-green summer dress with a black jersey and black high-heeled shoes. She took long, confident strides up the dusty street towards us, but then suddenly stopped as if something had got her attention.

"Momo!" she yelled out to someone we couldn't see from where we were standing. Then, from out of the house in front of her, came Moipone, hurrying towards her mother, her hair flowing behind her and her blouse blowing in the breeze. Her mother put down the parcel she had in her hands, adjusted the strap on her handbag and then spread out her hands to receive her daughter, kissing her before she enveloped Moipone in her arms.

For some reason I couldn't move my feet. Ole was about six steps ahead of me when she turned around and called me to keep going.

"What's wrong?" she asked, but it took me a moment to realize what she had said. I shook my head and started walking to her—and towards them.

I stared and stared, with a furrowed brow and my mouth wide open, through the introduction to Moipone's mama, who said hello with gentle eyes but no smile. I looked past Moipone and saw that she had been sitting with Basi, Kgosi and two other girls who I didn't recognize. I would have kept staring without saying anything had Ole not nudged me and repeated, "What's wrong?" at which point I cleared my throat, shook my head and said, "Hello," too late, to Moipone's mother.

It wasn't until I was home and lying in my bed with the light turned off listening to the calming voices of Boyz II Men singing "End of the Road" that it came to me, as slowly as the music and just as poignantly: Moipone's mother didn't just love her the way most mothers love their children. She wholeheartedly *adored* her. My mother never held her arms out to me like that, she rarely kissed me and she hardly ever called me by my nickname, Nedi. I had seen her hold her arms out like that, though. Of course I had. I had seen her give that kiss and that hug and that look of absolute delight. I just hadn't seen it directed at me.

It took what felt like forever for me to fall asleep. I had not been someone who had trouble falling asleep before then. In fact, most nights, I never even heard the end of the first song I played on my CD player. But that, I see now, was the beginning of many, many sleepless nights that have continued well into my adulthood. One thing became clear to me that night, quite forcefully, really.

It was what people meant when they said that it was a great day when my brother was born.

A great day for all of us, I kept thinking.

12

THE BIG SURPRISE the Saturday of Basi's game was not the fact that Papa came. He rarely made it to Basi's games because he was working, but I had known that he was planning to come to this one.

The big surprise was that Moipone and Kgosi were there. Well, Moipone more than Kgosi. Many times Basi had gone to watch Kgosi's school soccer matches—Kgosi played soccer because he went to school in the location, where they didn't have what were known as "White" sports like rugby or cricket. Even I had gone sometimes with Ole and we had all watched him together while eating *sephatlho* and drinking Stoney on the sidelines in the heat.

We didn't see them when we arrived at the school and they hadn't come with Basi. Basi had been at his school early with his team, getting a pep talk from their coach, who was also the sports teacher. We had all gone in Papa's car and dropped him off there first.

Basi was very excited that morning when he got ready. The rest of the house was buzzing nervously around him, running around looking for this and that: "Where are your socks?" "What do you want to eat?" "Basi, shouldn't you eat something?" But Basi had shown no nervousness whatsoever.

I was disappointed when I realized that of course Kitsano would not be there because he was still in Botswana, but he had remembered it was the day of the big match and had phoned about twenty minutes before we left. Mama had given the phone to Basi, and Basi, thankfully, had given it to me.

"Howzit?" came the deep voice through the phone that had me collapsing onto Basi's bed. Basi had the privilege of a phone in his room, installed as a gift when he turned sixteen.

"Your brother must be stoked," he said slowly in his confident-sounding voice. Why was it that boys were never as nervous around girls as we were around them?

I was nodding furiously and grasping the duvet cover on my brother's bed when I realized that I was required to speak.

"Ja . . . ," I said finally. My legs felt wobbly. "He's excited. We're *all* excited," I added a little too loudly. "So . . . how's Botswana?" I managed to say.

Mama yelled, "Naledi, off the phone! We have to go, now!"

I crossed my legs and clasped the phone tighter with my now sweaty hand.

Kitsano said, "You have to go?"

"Umm . . . yes. But . . . um . . . not now." I was trying to sound cool but knew that I wasn't quite managing.

"Botswana's OK. It's OK. Lots of relatives . . . " There was an uncomfortable pause. "So . . . two weeks, huh?"

"Yes! Two weeks," I said, shutting my eyes tightly with the realization that I sounded much too excited.

Kitsano gave an easy laugh.

"I look forward to it," he said.

When we were all hurrying into the car, Mama stopping to examine what she thought was a scuff mark on her shoes, Papa patting his pockets for keys, and me clutching my stomach to calm the butterflies, I was struck with the distinct and embarrassing feeling that I had no impressive skills in speaking to boys.

As we sped toward the highway I remembered what Limakatso had said to me that week in school: "You know he'll want to take the next step, right?" The next step. We'd hardly even been on a date. We'd only kissed that time at the social, and seen each other next when Mama and I were picking up Basi from school. We were going out but hadn't really gone out. The matric dance was the next step. I was definitely not ready for the kind of step Limakatso was referring to, even less ready when she had offered her lesson on boys: "The thing is . . . when boys are ready, there's nothing you can do."

"We're almost there. Are you ready?" Mama's voice brought me out of my daydreaming. I think Papa must have sped to town because we had arrived sooner than I had anticipated. So much was going on! I couldn't find a comfortable point for my mind to rest on: rugby match, Moipone, Moipone's mother, Ole and Moipone, Kitsano . . . the "next step."

So when we finally settled down on the stands and I looked over to my left and saw Moipone and Kgosi arriving, I was floored. I thought: *This is risky. Mama is going to be so angry. Is Basi mad?*

He probably was. I didn't know if this was his way of telling our parents that he was in love and showing Moipone his world at the same time. For a moment I imagined that maybe Kgosi had planned to come and had decided to bring Moipone as a surprise, to cheer Basi on. But I knew of course that that was ludicrous. What did Kgosi ever do without Basi knowing about it?

So I sat up straight as the two of them walked towards me, and I waved. Then I put my hands underneath my thighs to stop from fidgeting. I noticed as they slowly approached that Kgosi, looking as comfortable as if he went to rugby matches all the time, was wearing a Kaizer Chiefs cap, which I knew he had done to be funny.

Moipone, in a short blue skirt and white blouse, sat next to me, so that I was to her right and Kgosi to her left.

"Hello," she said confidently.

"Hello. Ah, Kgosi," I said, pointing to his hat. "I like your *kepisi*."

"Sure, *jo*," he said, nodding and not smiling. "Where's Basi?" He looked over the crowds.

I pointed as Basi's team arrived in a small bus that parked just outside the school gates. Out they came, running over to the field, looking ready and excited.

People started cheering and clapping. I heard Mama's voice yelling, "*Heeee*, Basiiiiiiiiii!" She was sitting in front of me with Papa and some of the other team members' parents and after she cheered, she turned and gave me a what-are-those-two-doing-here look. I shrugged and hoped, really sincerely hoped, that neither Kgosi nor Moipone had seen that.

Moipone put her fingers gently on my knee to get my attention.

"Is he the only Black guy?" she asked in Setswana.

I looked around, taking deep breaths to get over my nerves.

"No. This is just the first team. There are two other teams."

She was sitting so still, her hands clasped on her knees and her legs crossed. She looked quite composed.

"So . . . there are a few Black guys in the school. He's just the only one on the team," I said.

"He could go far. He could go on to be one of the first Black guys on the national team in a few years. If he is chosen," she said.

I nodded.

"So where are the other Black guys? Why aren't they on the team?"

"Uh . . . " I licked my lips and looked at my watch just to do something with my hands. "He's the only one in the first team. I don't know . . . Basi says it's hard to get chosen." That didn't really answer the question. It never did for me.

Both teams ran over to their respective coaches and I had to speak above the excited cheering.

"He thinks that'll change . . . ," I said, shrugging.

She nodded, more because she had heard me than because she was impressed with anything I said.

Basi had always said it didn't make sense. His only explanation was, "You have to remember these schools only opened for us recently. These other guys have been playing rugby for much longer. They've been on teams much longer." Even he didn't seem completely satisfied with his own answer.

"Still . . . ," I'd say to him sometimes.

"Ja. Still . . . I mean, a lot of the Black guys are good. I mean really, really good . . . but the coach is tough, man!" he'd laugh. He felt very loyal towards his coach.

Just then there was some confusion. The coach of the other school marched over, taking hurried and furious strides towards Basi's coach. He beckoned with his hand as he approached, and Basi's coach skipped over to him, the whistle around his neck bouncing up and down his chest.

Nothing seemed seriously amiss, so I looked over at Moipone and thought I may as well start getting to know her while we waited.

"Which school do you go to?" I asked.

"Marapong High."

I nodded. "Hoh! Are you and Kgosi in the same class?"

"Ja." She looked over at him. "He's always making the class laugh, this one," she giggled.

"Are you and Ole good friends?" I thought she'd look startled by this because we hadn't been speaking about Ole at all. But she didn't. She laughed softly again. She didn't raise her voice above the noise, so I had to lean over to listen more closely.

"Ja." She took out her Lip Ice and rubbed it on her lips. "Is she your best friend?" she asked.

"Ja," I said. "Sort of."

"She likes to take care of people, Ole. She has a lot of friends at my school."

This made me feel uneasy—I knew I didn't have as many friends in Kasi as Ole and my brother did.

Moipone put the Lip Ice back in her small bag. "She shows me around, tells me who to stay away from. She's like a big brother." Here she looked away and over at the field. She cleared her throat. "Except she's a girl," she added.

It was awkward then. People didn't know how to talk about Ole. They called her a boy all the time. Those who didn't know her, with a little malice in their voices, would call her "Transie." "Why does she want to be a boy?" they'd ask.

I wanted to ask Moipone all kinds of questions. But right at that moment what I really wanted to know was if she understood that Ole didn't want Moipone seeing her as a sibling.

There was a commotion on the field. The game was about to start and I was nervous. I was always nervous at Basi's games. There was always someone on the sidelines yelling some profanity at my brother. At home he would tell me to watch closely and see how he was targeted on the field; some guy was always yelling things like "Get the Kaffir!" It was horrible, but he was used to it, he told me. It was a rough game, rugby. Just rougher for him.

Basi's coach ran back to his team and threw his hands up in the air. He spoke to his team for a minute and they all talked amongst themselves, a few shrugging, shaking their heads.

We saw Basi turn around and walk back to the bench.

Mama stood up and so did Papa. "Basi?" she called out.

For a second I thought he was just going to fetch something, but then he picked up his rugby bag and started walking away from the field. Behind him the teams ran towards each other, the whistle blew and the match started.

Without him.

Moipone, Kgosi and I tore down the steps of the stands two or three at a time, following my parents, who were running after Basi.

We could hear people asking, "What's going on?" "Why isn't he playing?" "Is he sick?" Then as I got to the last step, I heard someone say, "He's probably having a tantrum. You know these Black guys."

"My brother doesn't have tantrums!" I yelled in the direction of the voice.

I saw Basi put his bag in the boot of Papa's car and then open the back door to get in.

We ran the length of the field, my parents getting to him first. But before Moipone, Kgosi and I got there, Mama let out a scream, passing us as she ran back and onto the field, interrupting the game.

The players stopped. Some shouted at her to get off the field.

I saw her yelling and pointing at the coach, who stood still and seemed to do nothing but shrug his shoulders and spread his hands out helplessly.

13

IT WAS A LONG ride home. No one spoke in the car.

When we got home the first thing Basi did was hurl his rugby bag across the floor. We stood behind him and watched it slide across the kitchen and land in the middle of the passage. Then he marched to his room and slammed the door behind him. This was the angriest I had ever seen him. About five minutes later he walked out of his room and Kgosi, now alone, suddenly arrived at our door ready to whisk my brother away.

My parents and I were standing around in the kitchen trying to find something to do, waiting for Basi to talk to us, when he walked right through the kitchen, out the gate and down the road to Kasi, where he was to stay until much, much later that night.

When I think back, I wish I could erase the two weeks that followed. I'd like to change the story so that after the rugby match that didn't happen, we could skip over the next two weeks and go straight to the matric dance. Then we'd be done with it. It would have been difficult, I know, to have a nice dance after that match, but I like to believe we would all have gotten through fine if nothing else had happened.

That my brother and I would still be close.

That my feelings about him would still be simple.

I like to imagine that there are people in the world for whom uncomplicated truths remain. These people may go to the end of their lives without having these truths tested—without ever losing a grip on the things they've always counted on. Without feeling that deeply disconcerting sense of their world crumbling around them.

I am not one of those people.

What happened at the game? Basi got to school on time. He met his team, who were fired up and excited. Their coach gave them a slightly more charged pep talk than usual. They patted each other on the back, and said "Let's go get them!" and whatever other things teammates say to each other before a game. They then proceeded to get into the bus and sing morale-boosting songs all the way to the other school, where they saw their parents and friends excitedly waiting for them. They waved to everyone. They got on the field and had another pep talk.

Then the surprise: the other team declared they wouldn't play with the Black guy. Infuriating? Yes. Surprising? Not if you'd heard all the stories we'd heard. Basi was used to getting unfairly put out of a game, but this was the first time he was refused a chance to play at all. What did his team do? They shrugged and said, as Basi told me, "Too bad, mate," "Ja, it's tough because the selectors are here," and, "This is a big one, mate." They'd shaken their heads. "We can't shut this game down." And in the end, simply put, they got on with their game.

"I'm the captain. I've stuck my neck out for a lot of those blokes," he later said—more to himself than to me.

"Why didn't the coach say anything?" I asked—and this I still wonder about.

Basi, at this, shook his head. It's the closest I've seen him come to crying.

14

THE WEDNESDAY THAT AUS' NONO, Kgosi's mother, came home was the first sunny day after four straight days of rain. In Marapong this was unusual both because it was now April and because we normally had quick and furious thunderstorms that lasted, at most, thirty minutes.

Not that week. That week didn't feel right from beginning to end. The first day of rain was that Saturday of my brother's rugby match. The following Saturday was the hideous incident.

In the week following the match I could see that Basi was determined to pick himself up, dust himself off and walk away unscathed.

"I've always known who my brothers are," he told me when I asked about what his teammates had said when he'd seen them at school on Monday. "I'm not interested in those guys' bull."

He'd asked the rugby coach if he could be excused from matches for the rest of the season, and when he was not allowed to quit—because the coach insisted it had been the team's decision for Basi not to play the other school, and that it was "just one game"—he feigned illness all week. Dr Moeng, Papa's friend whose surgery was just behind our shop, wrote to the school at Papa's request and said that Basi had a problem with his knee that would not allow him to play rugby in the foreseeable future. That was the end of that, for rugby. Neither

Basi nor my father wanted to talk about it. It didn't stop me and my mother from asking questions though.

"I'm proud of him for showing them this is not the end for him," my mother told me one day as we were finishing up at the shop. "He's going to be someone big and rugby . . . " she pursed her lips angrily and shook her head, " . . . heh-eh, rugby is not everything. They do this to Black guys all the time." She was clearing the table in the office too hastily, her hand moving furiously across the surface, picking up things and putting them back down. "There'll never be a Black guy on the national team—and now we know why. First hand."

But Basi seemed to move on. There was the dance coming in two weeks. His finals were in six months and his studies at UCT, Rhodes, or Wits—he still couldn't decide which—would start in less than a year.

I thought with deep regret of how much I would miss him; how much my life at home would never be the same. No one would stand up for me when Mama was angry. I wouldn't sit in his room and listen to stories about *ko motseng*. I would have to go to socials without my protective older brother. I felt nothing but dread at the thought of Basi being out of the house, even though I knew how much of his life had been leading up to this: the beginning of his path to greatness, like other honourable women and men who had gone into law and changed our country. I understood what it meant to him to become a lawyer because he talked so much about it—about Kgosi's mother and all those women unjustly imprisoned.

So in the end, when it all happened, it wasn't that I was jealous and had "never wanted him to succeed," as Mama later put it.

———— ◈ ————

It started with the end of the rain, a strange heatwave and, most importantly, Kgosi's mother's release. It was quite an unceremonious homecoming, at first: there was barely mention of it in the location. People felt rather ambivalent. No one really knew how to look her in the eye. A woman accused of murdering her husband doesn't inspire praise poetry, I suppose.

Basi, on the other hand, was very excited at her release and anxious to be with Kgosi every step of the way. He wanted to be there when she came out and, unbeknownst to our parents, had arranged to meet Kgosi after school so that they could go to the jail together. He told me this and insisted with a very serious wagging of the finger that I not say a word.

"Not even to Ole," he said, looking me in the eye.

"I don't tell Ole what you tell me." I was offended by the suggestion.

"I just mean no one, Nedi. No one." Then he added as an afterthought, "Ole loves to talk."

I looked away. I would later understand, very painfully, what he meant.

He asked Papa if he could stay away from the shop because, as he put it, Kgosi needed him. I think Papa knew—because he knew everything that went on in Kasi through his employees and his friends who were lawyers and knew about the case— but he didn't fight him on it.

It was a hot day when she came home, too hot for April. At school I had taken off my jersey, which I had worn in the morning because it had been cool, and tied it around my waist like a belt so that it brought up my school dress a little bit and showed off more of my thighs. Those of us swimming in the thrilling waters of puberty had found creative ways to bear the heat in our uniforms; one or two braver girls had even unbuttoned their dresses, risking the wrath of the teachers.

Mama came to fetch me first. When I climbed into the car she gave me her most disapproving look.

"Pull down your dress. *Bathong*, Naledi!" She waved her arm impatiently at me, her bangles chiming furiously. "Why do you make yourself look like you're hoping to find a man?" She clicked her tongue as she started the car.

I pulled down my dress a little bit, but she wasn't satisfied.

"Put that jersey back on. Look decent, please."

I didn't say anything in response and only tried to keep my face from looking defiant. In a few minutes we would see Kitsano, who was back, and I didn't want to be in a bad mood then. I had resolved not to let my mother upset me. I rolled down the window, pushed my seat back and closed my eyes, letting the breeze sweep over my face. Mama turned on her music and seemed to let it go as she sang along to the songs.

I saw Kitsano almost immediately: he was standing with Basi at the bottom of the steps that led to the school hall. Mama drove up so that they were on my side of the car, and Basi was already walking towards us before we came to a stop. I noticed that he didn't have his bag.

"Mama," he greeted. "Nedi, can you come and help me get my bags, please? I'm taking more things home."

I almost jumped out of the car and kissed my brother at that moment. Kitsano was standing behind him now, his hands in his pockets the only thing betraying how nervous he was.

"OK," was all Mama said as she pressed the button to open the boot.

Kitsano and I walked side by side a few steps behind Basi, whose stride became more hurried so that we were lagging far behind by the time we reached his class. He sort of disappeared then, giving us a moment to ourselves.

"How are you?" Kitsano said, his fingers brushing against the tips of mine as if deciding, before he held my hand firmly in his.

"OK," I said and grinned foolishly, trying not to giggle. Basi had told me that boys found giggling annoying. "So . . . do you have a dress yet? I hear all the girls have been rushing around trying to catch their breaths . . . hoping to get the best dresses in town."

I was charmed by how he sounded like an American teenager, pronouncing the "r" in girls and saying things like "in town." Some people from Lesotho and Botswana did that. They would go to international schools, where they mixed with Americans and then they would come out with American accents. Usually I found it annoying, but not this time.

Basi came out of the room carrying two large sports bags. He handed me one without saying a word and then started walking towards the car. As soon as he turned the corner Kitsano said, "Let me take that," and took the bag from my hands. As he did, he leant forward and brushed his lips against mine. My knees went wobbly and I held onto his arm for support.

"It's good to see you," he said, wrapping his arm around my waist.

I pressed my body against his and felt all of him against me. When he finally let me go I realized that the world had gone completely quiet.

By the time we were back at the car I was trying not to grin too much.

Kitsano put the bag in the boot and winked at me as he walked away.

"I'll see you on Saturday."

I really, really, like him, was all I could think on the way home. *I wonder what else we'll do at the dance.* I hardly noticed anything or anyone even though I stared out of the window the entire time.

I *really* liked him.

15

WHEN BASI CAME HOME from the prison he was subdued but not exactly sad. I sat on his bed with him while he told me about it. It was nice to see Aus' Nono come home, he said.

"She cried when she saw Kgosi standing outside waiting for her. It was really sad, but also really nice." He was lying on his back with his knees up and I was sitting near the edge of the bed, listening.

"I think we'll have a party on Saturday. Just a welcome-home thing. Nothing big." He closed his eyes, listening to his music—a mixed tape he had recently put together, with my input. The tree just outside his window was blowing in the breeze, the cool air making its way into the hot room.

"This is exactly what I want to do, Nedi," he spoke with his eyes closed. "You know, women like her don't get fair trials. People don't understand that men—our men, I admit and it's very hard for me—" Here he took a deep breath, opened his eyes and touched his chest with the palm of his right hand. "But it's all men—Black, White, Indian, Coloured—who hurt women and then the women have to defend themselves. Aus' Nono was in there because of self-defence. Bra Speed used to beat her up. I mean . . . I could tell you some really rough stories. Eish!" He closed his eyes again. I thought he was deciding whether or not to tell me.

"He hit her, right?" I was speaking with my voice low, trying to sound nonchalant.

Basi sat up, leaned against his headboard and stretched his

legs. He looked down at his hands.

"He did and . . . " He rubbed his face with one hand and then sighed deeply as if he were exhausted. "He did. He did."

"So, now she's home."

"Yes. Now she's home. Shouldn't have been in there in the first place, but she is home." His voice lifted and he slapped his knee. "And we're having a party!"

"Basi . . . aren't people a little . . . I mean, who is . . . Who will come to the party?"

Basi sat up straight and looked at me.

"Nedi, you don't know. People loved Bra Speed. We all did. Everyone is sad that he's not here. Everyone. But some people still love Aus' Nono. I mean, some people just think it was an accident. There's still a lot of speculation."

"Didn't she admit it?" I was piecing together things that I had heard over the years that she had been in prison.

"No. She never did. She always said it was an accident." He moved closer to me and held my arms. "Nedi, no one knows that it wasn't. This is the biggest secret. No one knows. People suspect, but she has always said it was an accident. She said she was cleaning his gun and shot him by accident. *Don't ever say a word otherwise. To anyone.*"

His grip got tighter and I swallowed hard. I could feel the seriousness of what he had just told me.

"People gossip, but they don't know for sure. If they did . . . I don't know if anyone would support her. People really loved him."

I nodded. I understood very well how much people loved Bra Speed, and how they would find it difficult to forgive Aus' Nono if she said that she had done it. I promised myself that I would never tell anyone what Basi had told me. Ever.

But now you know.

You have to know, because if I don't tell you this part then the next part would come out of nowhere. I've also sworn to myself that if and when I tell this story, I will tell the whole truth.

That afternoon—that Wednesday afternoon after the rain, after Aus' Nono's release—would be the last time that I spent a quiet, easy time in my brother's room. I would never go in again, sit on his bed again, share jokes the same way after that. That was the end of those easy, lazy hours that we would spend together.

It is another slice of time, another packable moment that I carry with me wherever I go.

16

WHAT HAPPENED NEXT? What do I remember? I know the answer so well. People tell you that memory is an unreliable ally. "We should never trust it wholeheartedly," was what my father once told me. "It's a tricky thing." I know that. I know it even better now, being almost fifteen years older. No one goes through their turbulent twenties without realizing that much of what they remember about their childhood is either embellished to get them through the difficult times or completely tucked away, for the same reason. My story—I mean, what I saw with my own two eyes—is neither, however. I never remember it differently. The details are never fuzzy, nor do they ever change. I have never had moments of thinking: *Was it a white blouse or a red blouse that she was wearing? Or: I can't think what colour her shoes were.*

Some may think that this is a sure sign that I am, in fact, lying. I once read that in war interrogations, the telltale sign of a liar is that their story never changes. No matter how much they are tortured, they stick to the same lie, step by step, detail after detail. Could I have put one story in my mind and refused to allow the natural workings of memory over time to interfere? Of course I've asked myself this. Of course I have! This is my brother's life; it was *my* family whose livelihood was to completely disintegrate if I said anything. So yes, of course I've asked myself if maybe I was getting something mixed up. Even more importantly, I've had moments of wondering if maybe, just maybe, there is a possibility that I misunderstood. Although

I must admit that these moments have been few and far apart. I'm ashamed to admit this fact: that I give my brother the benefit of the doubt very rarely on this one. But then . . . well, shame is a constant companion, isn't it? A ball of steel chained to my ankle.

The party for Aus' Nono had gone remarkably well. Mama had forbidden us to go, but Papa had insisted that it was "just a party," and that, really, it would be rude not to be there.

"It's for Kgosi," he had told her after taking his last spoonful of ice cream one evening. "It's not for Nono. It's for her son. Basi is like his brother. If he doesn't go, this will be very sad."

So Mama had relented, and we had gone.

My first impression of Aus' Nono was how frail she looked. I had remembered her being a solid woman with round hips and large hands that she was always waving in the air as she talked. At that party she looked tired, thin, and was mostly quiet while the singing and the drinking and the eating went on around her. I didn't go over to greet her because she was surrounded by her friends, people my mother's age, and it would be rude to go and sit among adults. Mainly I kept my distance, sitting under a tree in Kgosi's backyard while Basi and Kgosi ran the show, giving people drinks and making sure everyone had enough to eat.

I remember getting a very good sense of how close Basi was to Kgosi's mother. I mean, when we were younger and living *ko motseng* I knew that Kgosi's mother really loved my brother. She had treated him like a second son. Sometimes when she came home from work after getting paid she would give Basi and Kgosi little presents, like a spinning top or a ball. Mama had never liked it, although she did the same for Kgosi then, possibly not wanting to be outdone. Ole, who had often

observed this, called it "the battle of who loves their son more."
Now it appeared that in spite of the prison bars Aus' Nono
and Basi's bond had stayed strong. I understood why Basi
had gone with Kgosi for visits, why he was so gutted by her
experience.

At the party, he kept walking over to where she was sitting
and handing her plates of food. He ran back and forth making
sure she had a glass of water or ginger beer. At one time I saw
her take his hand between both of hers and pat him lightly,
then cup his chin, the two of them laughing together. From
a distance—if you didn't know anything—you would have
thought she was his mother.

I was with Ole, who was sitting with her legs apart drinking
Coke from the bottle, bobbing her head to the music and
watching Moipone's every move.

"When did you become good friends?" I asked her.

She only gave a noncommittal shrug.

"So," she said, shifting her weight and adjusting her hat
unnecessarily, "I still haven't seen the dress."

"Come and see it later," I said, perking up and getting
animated with my description of the dress. Ole, I knew, had
no interest in the dress. She was feigning interest in me and
my excitement about the dance, while occasionally darting her
eyes towards whatever corner Moipone was occupying.

Basi unhooked his arm from around Moipone's neck so he
could go and sing along with Kgosi, and Ole's face brightened.
She leaned forward as if about to stand, then steadied herself
and pretended she was only stretching.

Basi and Kgosi—along with a few of their friends, beer
bottles and cups in their hands—stood up to dance and sing
along to Arthur's "Kaffir": *Don't call me a Kaffir . . . Hei Baas . . .*

Ole sat back in her chair then and watched with her legs
stretched out. Staring but pretending not to from under the

brim of her hat, she started biting her nails when Basi went back to where Moipone was sitting, linking his fingers with hers and pulling her to stand up.

"Isn't it funny how these guys act like they relate to some American ghetto reality?"

I shrugged and forced a smile. I had seen Ole's eyes do this, this look of resentment when someone had rubbed her up the wrong way. I had also seen that look directed at Basi and Kgosi. The two of them were some sort of thorn at her side.

When M'Du started howling "Siya Jola," Basi and Moipone moved together to the centre of the dance circle. Five Bop danced his way out to make room for them. Ole put her elbows on her knees and clapped her hands, bobbing her head to the music with her eyes closed, refusing to see Basi and Moipone dancing in the middle of the circle, his hands on her hips. Basi had eyes for no one else.

I stood up and went to join in the dancing.

"*Ayeye*, Bafana!" I heard Fezile, one of Basi and Kgosi's old Kasi friends say. "*Di a bowa!*"

That prompted some laughter, and I could see how perfect it seemed to everyone, including me. The boys were all as infatuated with Moipone as Basi was. I mean, really, just her calm eyes took your breath away. Later, when Ole went on about "the idea of her," I never protested because that was one part of it that I understood.

I thought we would be there all afternoon, but soon after Basi came over and told me that it was time to go. I was surprised because it was early, especially considering that Basi was one of the hosts. He and Kgosi had driven food and drinks from the shop with Papa's approval. They had organized this together— probably for longer than any of us realized.

Ole stood up and shook Basi's hand with a smile—I think because she thought we were leaving and Moipone wasn't. But we soon saw that Basi had other plans. Ole walked us to the car, and before I could climb in Basi said, "Can you sit in the back?" in English and in a whisper.

Ole looked behind us and frowned. Out came Moipone in her short denim skirt, black clogs, and a flowy white top with thin straps. She had tied her hair back so that you got the full effect of her perfectly made-up face and no one—I mean *no* one—could help but stare at her flawless skin, her full lips and her big, round eyes.

She smiled at me without showing her teeth and climbed in the front seat of the car. Then she quickly stepped out and gave Ole a hug before going back in. I didn't look at Ole. I willed myself to look away. The innocence of Moipone's hug had cut through me and I knew without seeing her face that it wasn't what was supposed to happen. Even I felt the sting when my brother cheerfully said, "Sharp, Ole!" then stopped and asked politely, "Do you want to come with us? You could sit in the back with Nedi?"

Ole stepped back and folded her arms across her chest. Her hat covered her eyes. I kept mine on the floor of the car. I fiddled with my already-fastened seat belt as my brother sped off, leaving Ole in a rather offensive cloud of Kasi dust.

When I turned around, I saw that she was walking, quite slowly, head down and with hands in pockets, away from the party towards her house.

At our house Basi left Moipone and me to sit in the back garden while he went to fetch us something cold to drink. The sun was moving further west, but it would still be another hour or so before dusk.

Moipone and I sat on the large brown blanket that I had laid on the lawn, and chatted while we waited. I noticed that Basi was taking quite a long time. Maybe putting on more cologne? I chuckled at the thought and Moipone turned to me with a questioning look. I just shook my head. She stared at the fountain with a slight smirk on her face. She leaned on her elbows, and I did the same. I noticed that she had much bigger breasts than I did, and that her skirt was even shorter than I had realized. I envied her for being allowed to wear it.

"My mother would never let me wear a skirt that short," I told her. I immediately regretted it when she frowned at me. "I like it," I added. "My mother never lets me wear anything short."

She smiled.

"How long have you and Basi been going out?" I asked her.

She smiled sweetly, then shrugged. I didn't quite know what I wanted to hear from her—but I did have this need to be accepted. I wanted to say something that told her I was just one of the girls, not this stuck-up girl who lived in diEx and went to school in town and spoke English in Kasi.

"My boyfriend and I—you'll meet him at the dance—we—"

"You have a boyfriend?" She grinned and looked me up and down.

I felt a bit embarrassed. My voice came out too high. "Yes!"

"You're allowed?"

I giggled in spite of myself. "No. My mother doesn't know."

Moipone sat up straight and looked at me. "Boys can wait. You're too young," she said.

"Did you have a boyfriend when you were my age?"

She shook her head. "No."

"Your mama didn't allow it?"

She crossed her legs and smoothed her skirt as she smiled

thoughtfully. "My Mama asked. I wasn't interested."

I gasped. "Your mama asked?"

Moipone waved my question away. "She's not like a lot of mamas."

I could see that.

"You talk about everything?" I asked enviously.

Moipone nodded.

I started picking at the grass. "My brother really likes you, you know," I heard myself saying. What I really wanted to add was that I liked her too, without even knowing her. I wanted to say that she was beautiful. Stunning.

Remember when you were growing up and you were just old enough to have stopped playing *khati* or fish or *diketo*, and you would walk past little girls playing those games and they would say to you, "*Aus' o pila, waitse?*" I felt like one of those girls. Like I was seeing an older girl and wishing I'd have her looks and composure when I grew up.

I expected her to grin broadly the way other girls would— most girls at my school, in fact—if I told them my brother had even mentioned their names. But instead, when I looked up, I was surprised by the look of confusion that briefly crossed her face. Then I saw, when I looked behind me, that Basi had just appeared from the house. He didn't have cooldrinks in his hands but whatever he had, he swiftly tucked behind him when I turned to face him.

Moipone stood up and brushed some grass off the back of her skirt and Basi took her by the hand and led her to the back room.

I knew then.

I just knew what was going on, even though it took me a long time to realize what he must have been hiding behind his back when I turned around.

17

THE CRUNCH, CRUNCH of the pebbles between the house and the back room sounded their retreating steps and I stayed behind and stared at the fountain. I was feeling a bit disappointed that I was not going to be chatting with Moipone longer. For some reason I had imagined that the three of us would be sitting together sipping cooldrinks until the sun went down.

I was walking to the kitchen, thinking that maybe I would go in and phone Kitsano, when I heard the song coming from the radio in the back room. It sounded like Tracy Chapman's "Baby Can I Hold You," and I started to laugh because I was surprised that Basi had it on the mix tape. I had insisted that he put it on, since he didn't like Tracy Chapman, so when I turned around I was only going to share a laugh with him about it— say "Haha, you do like her," maybe, and that was all.

I had one foot up on the top step leading into the house, but then I—*regrettably*—changed my mind. I say regrettably because, quite honestly, I would give everything precious in my life to have made a different decision. I can't tell you how many times since that day I have tried to will myself, in retrospect, to *just go into the house*. Go into the house, phone Kitsano, take a bath, fantasize about the matric dance.

I would be writing a very different and much more pleasant story if I had done just that.

I heard a raised voice saying "No!" Foolishly, I imagined that this was about the song, and I started hurrying towards the back room. I remember that in my mind I had a silly idea that

Moipone and I would laugh at Basi for playing it.

Ugh. I was thirteen.

I walked towards the back room to have a quick laugh and maybe a chat.

I didn't get past the window.

I see it now as if it's happening still. I see it every night in my dreams, or when I'm awake. I see it from the corner of my eye when I'm at my desk sometimes, trying to work. It appears unexpectedly when I'm going about my business, looking at the post or just hurrying out of the house, when I'm thinking about nothing but the weather or the shape of the moon. And when I'm thinking about my brother or my mother or Moipone. I watch TV and random images of an advert or a silly show morph into the scene in the back room so that I have to turn off the TV and shut my eyes. It's like a film that never stops rolling.

So ask me whenever you want, wherever I am. Ask me any day of the week, at any time, when I'm awake or dozing off, when I'm busy and when I'm not. Ask me and I will tell it to you, exactly like this. For me this is not as much a memory as it is a scene I am constantly watching as it plays over and over again:

There they are, on the bed. She in her blue-denim skirt and white top and he in below-the-knee shorts and a black T-shirt with the white face of a lion on the back. It is a new T-shirt that he and my mother bought recently after he won a tennis match. My brother always has been a sharp dresser but he makes even more of an effort these days, wearing his newest or best clothes when he goes to see Moipone.

There is a perfect red rose on the bed, which he must have picked from Mama's garden, and which must have been what he was holding behind his back.

Wow. Romantic, I think.

Years gone by and still; Words don't come easily, sings Tracy.

Moipone pushes him and my brother pulls her. And at first it seems like a game. I think I even see them smile at each other. He cups his hand at the back of her head and pulls her face towards him, then she allows him to kiss her for a second before she pulls back. He puts his other hand under her top, and then the hand moves over her breasts, caressing them slowly. Then she takes the hand out and pulls down her shirt to cover her stomach. He puts his hand up her skirt and she pulls it out and crosses her legs. Then he lies down on his back and pats the space at his side, saying, "Come here."

I can hear him. I hear and see everything because I am looking through a window and the window is open and the curtains don't obscure my view. They hide nothing.

She looks down at the space and says, "No. I should go home. My mother's waiting. I have to cook tonight."

Baby, can I hold you tonight . . . Maybe if I told you the right words, ooh, at the right time . . .

He hears nothing she says, it seems, because he runs his fingers up her leg, and then pulls her close to kiss her neck. She tries again to push his hand away, but this time he grabs her thigh and she can't push it away. She starts to stand up but he pulls her back down. She starts again and again he pulls her back down.

It stops looking like a game.

He pushes her onto the bed and pushes her skirt up. She slaps him hard, repeatedly and vigorously with both hands, but he doesn't move—in fact, he barely flinches.

I don't think she has a chance.

His one hand is busy pulling down her panties and his other one is pushing down her wrists. She is wriggling and he keeps saying, "Ssshh . . . ssshh, I won't hurt you. I love you, I won't hurt you. Shhh, it's not painful. It's not painful. I've done it before. You'll like it. It's not painful." His voice is a very strange cross between soothing and commanding. He is moving with a brutish force that I have only seen in him when he plays sports. He is so focussed, unaware of anything else around him. His eyes narrow as if he is facing an opponent in a game—or a fight. He seems unaware of her even as he places his hand firmly over her mouth. His face is up, looking somewhere above her, behind her. He doesn't even take off his pants, just unbuttons his buckle and is swiftly on top of her, his hand still on her mouth.

"Ssshh . . . sshh . . . nnnn . . . nnnnn . . . shush . . ."

I love you . . . Is all that you can say . . .

Her cries of protest have now stopped. All she does is give the quick, low grunts of someone in pain. Her eyes are tightly shut, her arms still pinned down by my brother's left hand, but now her face turns—his right hand still on her mouth—and she faces my way.

Is she now suddenly aware that they are not the only ones here?

She looks at the open window, past the blue curtains billowing in the evening breeze, and her eyes land on me.

She is silent and still. I don't move. I only stare. She looks as if she has given up. She is not crying or moving or doing anything.

"Ssshh . . . shhh . . . aah . . . aaah . . . " my brother goes on.

She doesn't say a word. The lion moves up, down, up, down, up, down.

It could roar, I think. *It looks alive.*

Baby, can I hold you tonight . . . Maybe if I told you the right words, ooh, at the right time, you'd be mine . . .

I promise you, I tried to move. But my legs may as well have been immersed in cement. I just couldn't do anything.

Did I stay because I wanted to see? With all my heart, no . . . I don't think I wanted to see. At first, maybe. But I think in the end I couldn't do anything *but* see. I couldn't move. I really couldn't.

Then the gaze in Moipone's eyes rises, detaching, and moves up around the room, looking somewhere past me, then slowly, absently, coming back and settling on me. She seems to actually look at me, but then she turns her face again and her cheek, being close to the rose, is pierced by a thorn. My brother, seemingly unaware, pushes her face further down onto the thorn, creating a long, deep cut as she shifts. She shuts her eyes tightly, and this is when I finally move.

I tiptoe away, my hand on my mouth to keep from screaming or crying or yelling.

I walk back into the house, careful not to make a sound.

I ran into the bathroom and filled the basin with water. I steadily held onto the edges of the basin and leaned forward, immersing my face in the ice-cold water. I let it completely cover my face and didn't care about my hair, so that my lips and nose were touching the bottom of the basin.

I turned my face, let the water sting my open eyes. I stared, watched the water float around me, felt it go into my ears and heard only the soothing sound of bubbles while one ear was pressed against the cold ceramic. I turned the tap with one hand while the other held onto the edge of the basin for balance. I wanted to curl my whole body into a small ball and submerge it in that basin, disappear into the world of water, with no sound of screams or grunts of pain.

Sometimes in the night, when I start seeing them in the back room again, I wake up and I turn on the water and immerse my whole body—nightdress on or naked—into the solitary world of cold, comforting water. It's even more soothing than music. I can stay in there for a very long time, or until I stop thinking. I have spent entire evenings and the better part of many pre-dawn hours in cold baths with no sound, willing away my thoughts. I even missed a class or two at varsity—in those first few months when I was getting used to being away from home and living once again close to Basi.

That day, when I finally thought I could walk steadily again, I slowly came up for air. Without drying my head with a towel, I ran into my room and shut the door, locking it behind me. I climbed onto the bed and covered my head with a pillow, too shocked to cry.

Their footsteps pulled me away from the bed and I went to see what was happening. From my window I could see in the faint light of dusk Moipone hurrying home and my brother walking—not rushing—behind her. She was holding up her hand, pressing it against her chin. I wanted to tell her not to go that way alone, that it was getting dark. This is a feeling that has lasted all these years: me wanting to tell Moipone to stay safe. I wanted her to run away that night—to go as far away as possible—but couldn't stand the realization that it was my brother I wanted her to run from.

My brother, whose room and words and arms had always spelt safety for me.

Oh, I felt cold! Colder than a winter's night. My body was covered in goosebumps and my teeth clattered. I kicked off my shoes—saw them fly across the room and hit the pink wall, leaving a mark. I wrapped a blanket around me, then I climbed into bed without taking off my clothes. I lay face down with one pillow, then two, on top of my head, pressing down harder and harder, willing away my headache and making a salty puddle on my sheets with my tears. I never, ever, wanted to leave my bedroom again.

18

NEWS AND GOSSIP in the location spreads swiftly in all directions like tear gas on a Wednesday afternoon in the eighties. People always have their ears open for something new and as the saying goes: *Tsebe ga e na sekhurumelo.* Nothing goes unseen or unheard. And then it all gets thoroughly picked apart and examined around bonfires and kitchen tables, across fences and through the dust being agitated by a morning broom.

It was already dark when Moipone returned home that evening and, of course, many people saw her. I heard that her mother had been looking for her, frantically asking people at the party where she was as if she knew something was going on. Many, many people had seen Moipone get into the car with us; more specifically, they had seen Basi holding the door open for her as she *willingly* (they'd emphasize) climbed into the front passenger seat.

Long after the dust had settled it seemed the memory of her bare legs under a tiny skirt would linger in people's minds. Hardly anyone could tell you what my brother was wearing at that party. In fact, it has never been brought up by anyone since. I would even say that the only time I had an inkling that I was not the only person who noticed Basi's clothes was when Ole—in a fit of rage—said something like, " . . . and him in his black lion shirt . . . "

While I was hiding in my bed under large pillows, willing the memory away, Moipone was sitting on the sofa in her very small sitting room, crying to her mother about what had just happened. She told this to Ole, who later told me.

After Basi had walked Moipone home, he had gone back to the party. That he walked her home would later prove to be a crucial detail in the retelling of the story by witnesses—people who knew only that they had seen her getting into the car with us and then walking back home at dusk with him. According to them, Basi walked back into the party that evening, sat down with his friends and carried on until late, when Papa had driven over to fetch him and they had come back home.

"Now, you tell me who would do that if, let's say, something like that had happened?" was what Five Bop asked me two weeks later, in the heat of the ensuing debate, after the news had come out. "Not Basi," he said. "Not my brother."

"Not Basi" became the theme in subsequent weeks. "Not our Bafana."

When Papa and Basi arrived back at home I was asleep and I would stay asleep until early Sunday morning, when Mama woke us up so that we would get ready for the shop. On Sundays the workers were given the day off and the four of us managed by ourselves. It was always quiet at first as people woke up late or went to church; the noise and the bustle would increase towards the late afternoon, when they had had their Sunday lunches and were ready to go out and see friends and neighbours.

I didn't see Basi in the morning because he was still in his room when I left with Mama. I felt myself walking stealthily around the house, tiptoeing, avoiding his room with its closed door, which was just across the passage. I tried to calm myself as I moved through the usual morning routine, trying not to think about anything but what I was doing right then and there: *Take a bath; put your clothes on, one by one. Put your feet in your shoes; put the comb through your hair.*

In the car I looked out at the unusually quiet streets, at the lone Sunday-morning walker, the woman with a bag who was still going to work on a day when most people were resting, at the lorry filled with weekend vegetables, and I thought: *See. Nothing strange is going on here. It's fine. Whatever happened, I'm sure they'll find a way to talk about it. It's between the two of them.*

Mama and I drove through the quiet streets without saying a lot to each other. It was only when we crossed over to Kasi and saw Five Bop standing over a bowl of water outside his house, washing his face with no shirt on, that Mama said, "Was he at this party yesterday?"

I looked over at Five Bop getting ready for the day and wondered what he knew. I wondered if Mama had seen Basi before he went to sleep the night before, if she had thought something was terribly wrong with him or not. I looked over at her and saw no signs of concern, only that she seemed annoyed.

She shook her head with disgust. "I don't know when Basi will ever start living in his own world."

I turned away from her, opened the window and took the air in big gulps. *Tjo!* I was so tired. I felt exhaustion come in waves and overwhelm me at different moments during that whole day.

"What was it like, then?" Mama never had anything nice to say about Aus' Nono but she was always curious about her. She wanted to know everything that happened with her and was never impressed with any of it. The more she heard, the louder her tongue clicked and the more she pursed her lips with disapproval. But she kept on asking.

"Fine," I said, my face still turned the other way.

"What was she like? Nozipho? What was she like?"

I shrugged. "She looked fine," I told her. "Thin," I added. Mama adjusted her hands on the steering wheel. "Thin? *Mxm.* That's what happens in prison."

I didn't respond, only watched the houses with their windows and doors now opening, people stepping outside, sweeping their yards and getting ready for the day.

"She must have had a good lawyer. I can't believe that she's out already. What did Basi say about that? I'm sure he thinks they didn't let her out soon enough."

I turned around and looked at her. She looked me up and down as if daring me to contradict her.

"What did he say? Did he say, 'It's not fair! She deserves justice'?"

The only time that I ever heard Mama mocking Basi was in relation to Kgosi and his mother. Something happened to her when she thought about him with them. She came undone.

"He thinks she's innocent, you know?" she told me as we drove the car behind the shop. "Ha! Or maybe not innocent but justified. *Heeee. Iyo,* Basi! My child."

She was shaking her head as she picked up her bag and furiously climbed out of the car. I thought her hand was shaking when she pulled the key from her bag, put it to the lock and turned it.

"What does he tell you?" she was asking as we started our opening ritual, turning the alarm off and the lights on. "Hmm? What does he tell you?"

I didn't say anything because I didn't think she was really interested in my answer. I walked around to let her speak without me getting in her way. She was getting angrier and angrier, moving things around she didn't really need to, dusting shelves while I mopped the floors.

"These people are not like us," she ranted. "They're just not. They never have been. Basi won't listen. Will he? No, he won't. Maybe if your father pushed him to stay away from them. Maybe then. But no, your father won't do that. He grew up with Kgosi's parents. He was friends with Nozipho in high school, did you know that?"

I didn't.

"They were in the same class. She used to copy his homework. They used to be best friends. They haven't seen each other since he married me. I told him, after we're married, no more." I remembered him at the welcome party but didn't want to fan the fire.

At some point Basi and Papa walked in. As soon as I heard the door close I felt my heart race and I dreaded the moment my eyes would have to meet my brother's. I kept my head down then, mopping harder and longer than was necessary. But apparently I didn't need to worry.

"Eish!" I heard Basi's voice from behind me. "That party was great! I went to bed so late, I can't believe I had to wake up and come here this morning."

When I turned around he was carrying boxes of tea and packing them on the shelf. He kissed my forehead the way he often did when he saw me.

"You should have gone back with me . . . ," he was saying. He went on talking but I hardly heard any of it because I was staring at him, at his mouth moving and his hand stroking his head. He smiled and shrugged the way he did sometimes in the middle of telling a story.

" . . . and Five Bop was grabbing the beer . . . We just laughed at that . . . "

None of it made sense. It all came into my ears in strange little bursts.

I didn't know what to say, so I forced smiles and nods, forcing myself to stay in the moment and trying not to look anxious.

"You're mopping the same spot, Nedi," he said.

"Ah."

"Are you listening?"

"Ja! Ja, I'm listening."

"Did you sleep well? You look tired."

"Ja. I slept—"

Basi's hands were free; all the tea boxes were on the shelves. He was coming towards me and I felt my body stiffen. I kept my eyes on the floor, on his white tekkies with the large, black Nike swoosh. He reached over and put his arm around me, and his lips came and landed softly, gently, on my right temple. Just like that. Like it was just an ordinary day.

Then he pulled back, alarm on his face.

"Nedi, are you OK? Your face is hot. You're sweating."

My head was racing, trying to think of a lie. "I think you're right." My voice came out in barely a whisper. I started to walk around him, careful not to touch. "You should stay away. I think I may be getting sick."

"Mama!" I heard him yell behind me. "Nedi should go home—I think she's sick."

19

THERE WERE TWO DAYS left before the dance and I was wondering what happened between girls and boys in love— what I had always imagined versus the reality.

What did I know? Not much, apart from what I'd seen in films and on TV, where man and woman ended up happily and perfectly together, to the accompaniment of soft and romantic music.

Ole and I had had one or two conversations about her showing her breasts to boys but as she had often made clear, what boys did or didn't like was of no interest to her.

Limakatso was the most experienced of my friends, which really only meant that she had seen a naked boy. She used so many sexual innuendos that it was not always easy to understand her—and most of the time it was just too embarrassing to even ask her to explain.

At the time I don't know how far ahead I had thought. Not much past the kissing and caressing of the inner thigh, I think. A naked guy was roaming somewhere around the corners of my imagination, but I wouldn't say he was at the forefront.

But the closer we got to the dance, the more frightened I felt of being alone in the dark with Kitsano. What did people do before a night of high expectations? Did they phone each other or have a meeting where each established what the other expected?

Could I phone him and say casually, "Don't laugh, but my friend Kelelo thinks her date wants to have sex the night of the dance. What do you think? Haha!"

Who knew?

"Just a few more days, chommie!" Limakatso had said to me that Monday morning.

"Five!" squealed Kelelo.

The two of them screamed, holding on to each other.

I bit into my apple and only smiled in response. We were sitting on the lawn near the tennis courts with our legs crossed, eating our lunch.

Limakatso put her hands on my shoulders and shook me like she was bringing me back to life. "What's wrong?"

"I don't know, you guys." I tried for an acceptable lie. "I don't think I like my dress."

"I still haven't seen it," said Limakatso.

"Ja. I just know it's really, really nice," Kelelo chimed in.

"OK. Ja. It is, right?" *Iyo!* I could perk up at a moment's notice in those days.

"We'll love it!" Limakatso slapped me gently on the thigh. "Stop looking so gloomy and tell us about the kiss."

I cleared my throat.

"And how much sucking face you plan to do," Limakatso insisted.

"Yes!" Kelelo squealed. "What are you going to let him do?"

"Or should we say: What are you going to do to him?"

I laughed in spite of myself, and then I felt a rush of cold down my spine and a knot in my stomach.

"Hello! Tell. Now!" Kelelo was waving her hands all over the place. She could get really dramatic when she felt like it.

My friends were really excited for me to go on the big date. They wanted details, so I went on and on about the dress, trying to avoid thinking about the groping because the thought had suddenly occurred to me: *I don't really want to go any more. But I can't tell anyone.* Also: *I'm not supposed to know anything about what happened between Basi and Moipone. So I can't say anything.* Then the thought that weighed most heavily on me: *Did Moipone see me looking?*

Of course, by the middle of the week the stories had spread and there was fire and hell in the location. I learnt then that if you think people get angry when they feel wrongly accused, you haven't seen a person's rage when they think their child is wrongly accused. Point a finger at a woman and she'll hurt you; point one at her child and she'll kill you. The saying "*Mma ngwana o tshwara thipa mo bogaleng*" is not to be taken lightly. Not if you want to get out of the place alive.

Moipone—poor Moipone—was to learn this in the worst way.

I don't know what she said to her mother but I do know that they were awake for many hours that Saturday night, probably talking and crying. The light in their sitting room was the only one in the neighbourhood that was lit up all night—or at least it was still glowing at 2 am, when Ole woke up in her room and went to use the loo.

I also know that Five Bop had seen Moipone the following Monday morning as he stood at the side of the road waiting to wave down a taxi to take him to his first day at a new job in town. She didn't say "Ja, Five" when she walked past him; her shoulders were uncharacteristically slouched, and her tired eyes red and swollen. She had given him a little nod instead of stopping to chat. Everyone knew that he had finally got a job, and it had caused some bursts of celebration all around. But she had kept walking. Five recalled being a little bit annoyed. So he had yelled out "I'm going to work!" waving his white *scafteen* that carried a sandwich, an apple and a bottle of water. Moipone had politely turned around and responded " *O tsamae pila*" with a forced smile. Five had decided that there had probably been a death in the family and resolved to ask someone about it after work. In the meantime he had pointed his forefinger to the sky and let the eighteen-seaters zoom by as he waited for a sixteen-seater, until he realized that if he waited any longer then he would be late.

For me, the first sign that it was all about to go to hell came later that Monday afternoon. I was feeling rather exhausted, even though it hadn't been a particularly difficult day at school. I just had the sense of my heart being pressed down by a heavy hand. So I wanted to sleep, but I couldn't. I had to go to the shop and I thought of lying and saying I was still tired from the day before, but I decided it wouldn't be fair. There was a lot of stock coming in and my parents needed extra help in the office. So I left school with the driver Papa had sent to collect me.

The puzzling part was not that Basi had disappeared—he had gotten into the habit of disappearing—but he never missed important dates. The two of us always sat down with our parents and marked out on the calendar the days that the deliveries were made. It was crucial that we were there on those days. Basi was even friendly with half of the men who came to give us our monthly stock.

I was at the front counter, giving a customer her change and chatting about school—she was an old primary-school friend I recognized but whose name I couldn't remember—when I heard my father's thunderous voice reverberating through the store.

"Basimane! Is he here?"

I swallowed the gum I had been chewing and looked at Aus'

Johanna, who was packing cans of sardines into a blue plastic bag for someone. She looked back at me without stopping what she was doing.

We both understood the gravity of this. I turned to the girl I had been speaking to and said, "Sharp," and she said, "Sharp, Nedi," which sounded so sweet and familiar that I felt awful for not remembering her name. I turned back and shrugged at Aus' Johanna's questioning look.

Papa was pacing past the bread and biscuits section, his shiny black shoes matching the polished black floors.

I bit my lower lip and chewed as I rearranged the cigarettes and sweets behind the counter, and then bent down to repack the pads and tampons on the lower shelves. Aus' Johanna had asked me to speak to Mama about taking the tampons and pads from the toiletry section and placing them out of sight at the front counter. A few girls had made this request to her—there was always a woman working at the front counter, so they could be bought more discreetly. Aus' Johanna and I always placed them in a plastic bag below the counter before handing them to the customer.

As I put one box of Lil-lets on top of another, Papa screamed, "*O tlha kae?*"

I think that my body stopped moving. I knew that Basi had walked in, but he didn't respond. I remained squatting on the floor, looking at my reflection on the perfectly polished floor. A door slammed and someone's knuckles rapped on the counter above my head. I didn't—couldn't—move my legs.

"Sorry? *Askies? Aus'?*" someone called out.

The knuckles rapped again and a pair of heels clack-clacked impatiently.

I took deep breaths to collect myself. When I did finally stand up, I came face to face with Aus' Johanna.

"*Khante?*" she asked.

Before I could think of an explanation that wouldn't sound insane, Basi came out marching furiously from the office. He turned the corner, almost knocking over a customer, and disappeared through the doors. Papa followed Basi with just the same furious march and I think you could hear an ant move because the place was so quiet.

Most people in Kasi knew my father as a dignified, slow-walking man who politely asked about your family. So seeing him rush through the shop like that, his arms swinging and his tie loose, stunned everyone. Just when we thought they were gone, Papa and Basi came back into the shop and went directly to the office, both only a little bit calmer. People pretended not to stare but couldn't help it. Aus' Johanna and I busied ourselves with the customers, but we both strained our ears to hear what was going on in the office.

It took a very long time for them to come out of the room.

I was serving someone when Basi walked out, looking distraught. As he walked towards the door, Kgosi walked in, also looking sullen. I watched as the two of them huddled together, their heads bowed.

Aus' Johanna shook her head with relief.

"Ah, it's just boys. You know boys," she said, losing interest.

A moment later Papa came out of the office. Gravely, he shook Kgosi's hand, spoke briefly to the two of them and then gave Basi a set of keys.

For the first time, Basi turned to look in my direction and raised his hand to call me over. I reluctantly went to pick up my school bag from the office, thinking about how I had, so far, managed to avoid spending any time alone with him.

I needn't have worried. Kgosi stepped in at the front seat and neither one of them said a word to me.

We drove to Kgosi's house, where Basi turned the car off at the gate and said, "Let me go and greet your ma."

I waited in the back seat. When they had turned the corner of the grey brick house with the bright burgundy door and the shiny red stoep, I looked around the street and watched people without taking much in. Ole was nowhere to be seen, and for the first time it occurred to me how strange it was that Ole and I hadn't spoken that Sunday. It bothered me. I lifted myself off the seat and tried to get a good look at her house, the orange brick one with the bright green door and the red stoep, but there was no sign of anyone there.

I leaned further against the seat and closed my eyes. My heart felt so heavy that I wished to go to sleep right there.

But of course I couldn't sleep. Outside Kgosi's house, Basi and Kgosi came into view accompanied by Aus' Nono. They were deep in conversation, seemingly unaware of anything or anyone around them. At the gate Aus' Nono gave Basi a kiss on the cheek, and it looked to me like she was comforting him but I was too far to tell. Basi said something to her and then put his arm around her. She threw her head back and laughed, sending the other two into a chorus of laughter.

I knew I should get out of the car and greet, it being the polite thing to do, but I didn't want to move. Instead, I opened the window, and Aus' Nono seemed to notice me. I waved at her and managed a sizable and convincing grin, and she did the same. Then I forced myself into the front seat.

I watched the three of them standing there, looking like the perfect little family: a mother and her two very handsome boys doting on her. I preferred watching them from a distance. It was fascinating how they made sense as a threesome. Basi and Kgosi didn't exactly look alike, but they could pass as brothers.

The car was getting hot in the autumn afternoon; I wanted Basi to come back so that I could go home and lie in a cold bath.

"Nedi, you know you should have come out and greeted,"

Basi said when he had settled back into his seat. He was touchy about the way I behaved with Kgosi and his mother. I knew how upset he was when he continued, in English, "It's not . . . it's not OK, Naledi. Come on. Be respectful."

I thought: *I'd love to be completely immersed in water right now.*

He turned to look at me when we stopped at the corner of the street. His eyes softened and he sighed. "Sorry."

I shrugged.

"So. How was your day? I haven't spoken to you since—" His voice stopped abruptly as his eyes caught something in the distance.

Confused, I followed his gaze and saw it. Moipone and Ole, sitting on Moipone's front stoep. Sitting, I should say, very close together. I held my breath, dug my teeth into my thumbnail.

Basi took a deep breath and clenched his jaw. The softness in his eyes disappeared and he gripped the steering wheel and sped past the house, leaving the two girls in a mighty, vengeful cloud of dust.

He sped all the way through the location, bumping us through deep potholes and not stopping at stop signs, until he brought us to a frightening and violent stop in front of our garage, sending me lurching forward towards the dashboard. Without turning the car off, Basi opened his door and marched furiously out.

"The car key!" I called to him.

He marched back, turned off the car and yanked the keys out before proceeding to stomp like a sulking child into the house.

I ran after him, our feet crunching furiously on the pebbles. In the kitchen, Aus' Tselane stood wiping the kitchen counters and didn't smile to greet us the way she usually did. Without looking at her, Basi's hand went up, and when it came down it sent the keys flying across the shiny kitchen floor.

"Basi!" I yelled, but my brother was already gone and the

door to his bedroom was slammed shut.

Aus' Tselane didn't seem perturbed at all. There was such emptiness on her face that I had to look away. I wanted her to be stunned, horrified, upset even. She looked instead like a soldier eyeing a familiar horror. She clicked her tongue before turning around and going back to work.

I went straight to the bathroom, shut the door and locked it, and turned on the cold tap for a bath. Then I changed my mind and made it hot. When it was so hot that it was barely tolerable, I took off my clothes and left them on the floor. When I dipped my toe into the bath I felt some release.

I stayed underwater for as long as I could. Now and then I came up for air, and the house sounded quiet and serene. One time when I came back up, I heard Mama knocking furiously on Basi's door.

I immediately sunk back down.

20

"TELL ME YOUR DEEPEST, darkest secret." Ole spoke in a hushed tone coloured with a dark anger.

It was now the day before the dance and she was sitting in my bedroom while I got dressed, a ritual neither one of us was ready to abandon.

Ole sat on my window sill and watched the quiet road in front of our house. She was still and pensive, moving only when she brought the cigarette to her mouth and sucked in the nicotine. I stood behind her, nervously pulling on and taking off clothes. I hadn't spoken to Ole all week although I had seen her, of course, on that strange afternoon when my brother and I had driven past her and Moipone.

It had been a rather solemn week. The news of my brother and Moipone had seeped through Kasi like unidentified liquid from a rubbish heap.

"Aaah . . . " I pretended to be distracted. "We haven't played that in a while, have we?" I pulled on a little black dress and feigned deep interest in my figure as I stood in front of the mirror.

In the reflection, Ole turned her head slowly and her eyes pierced through me. I forced my gaze to stay on her.

"It's not a game," she said, her deliberately lowered voice without a hint of warmth.

My eyes turned sharply to the floor as I pretended to examine my shoes, desperate for somewhere else to look.

"Go on. Tell me." She stared at me through the mirror and

dared me to speak.

I smoothed my dress. Of course I knew what she was talking about. I knew what she had heard and I guessed what she and Moipone had been talking about that afternoon.

Five days before, I had been in the bath when I had heard Mama, clear as a bell, yelling, "What is this Moipone girl saying?" And I had been in the shop when I had heard Aus' Johanna saying to Mama, "Not Basi. I won't believe it. Sometimes girls do this to boys."

Let me go back a little, because this bit, where my conversation with Ole comes in, is rather harrowing. I'll get back to that.

The evening of Basi's strange and muted tantrum had been difficult. By the time I had come out of the bath, where I had been trying to hush my haunting thoughts, Mama, Basi, and Papa were sitting together in the sitting room. They were watching a football match and the commotion I had heard from the bath seemed to have completely disappeared.

Mama looked up from the brown leather sofa where she was sitting with her legs crossed and a glass of wine in one hand.

"Why such a long bath?" she asked, and I shrugged.

Basi moved over to give me room on the sofa. Football matches could be a fun family event, but this one was between teams no one really cared about, so I guessed that they were all just looking for a distraction.

I sat myself at the far end of the sofa and looked at the three of them: Mama in her royal blue tracksuit with her glass of wine in the hand with the sparkly gold bangles; Papa in his usual work uniform (a suit and a tie, now loosened); Basi in his long denim shorts, a white long-sleeved T-shirt that hung loosely over his shorts, and his white Nike tekkies.

I held on to a large red cushion that had been carefully

placed at the far end of the sofa. We had black leather sofas with a red-and-white carpet, red-and-white pillows and red-and-white curtains—my mother called it the "love theme" and had got the idea from *Femina* or *True Love*, I can't remember which. I clung to that scatter cushion like it was the last place of safety.

When an advert came on, Mama looked at me and said, "Do you know this Moipone girl?"

I nodded, then cleared my throat. "A bit. I've . . . " Here I looked at Basi and wondered what to say, but his eyes didn't meet mine. "I sort of know her."

"Is she a friend of yours?" Mama asked. She leaned forward and put her wine glass on the coffee table.

I looked at Basi again and still he didn't look my way.

"No . . . not really. Why?"

"Why?" She sat back, folded her arms across her chest and cleared her throat. She glanced at Basi, at Papa, and then back at me. "I think she has strange fantasies." She forced a brief and scornful laugh.

Visibly taken aback, Basi looked at Mama. I think he didn't know if he should smile or frown.

"Fantasies?" I asked.

Mama leaned forward, picked up her wine glass and held on to it as if it were a cup of hot chocolate on a winter night.

"Yes. What she wishes would happen. She's got *ditori*."

No one said anything as she took another sip of her wine, bangles chiming softly. She settled back into her seat.

"Let me tell you, I've had a terrible evening. First, I saw Vera—"

"The ghost?"

"Yes, Naledi. The ghost. I was driving home from the shop, just coming onto the main street from *lekeisheneng*, and there she was, running across the road. This is the first time that I've seen her alone. I mean, *I* was alone. Not her, she's always alone."

I shifted in my seat. Papa put off the volume on the TV as we all settled in to listen.

"She came straight towards me. Usually, you know," she looked at Papa, "she's crossing. Last time we saw her she was crossing the road, going from one side to the other."

"And I heard she's not always coming from the same side," Papa added gravely. "It could be *lekeishene* or *diEx*. She just runs." His finger flashed forward from behind his ear.

"Yes. So there I was, focussed on the road—I wasn't on my phone or anything—and I saw her coming towards me." She pressed her hand to her forehead like she was trying to stop a headache. "I nearly had an accident. I nearly drove into someone's house along the road. I was terrified. But as soon as I swerved, she was gone."

We all sat still and a rather sombre silence engulfed the room.

"Whose child is that girl?" Mama spoke with empathy, more to herself than to any of us, but it made me think about the people who had loved a lost daughter.

"Why is she called Vera?" I asked the room. "Does anyone know?"

Papa cleared his throat and spoke in a quiet voice. "There was a woman named Vera many, many years ago. When the location was still coming up. She was very beautiful, as the story goes. She was striking. People say that she disappeared after going out to buy vegetables on a Sunday morning."

"Some say she was just going to the dustbin to throw something out," said Basi.

"And some say that she was killed in her own house, but the body was never found. Her husband cleaned the place until it was spotless. So she runs around looking to go back home. Looking to get a lift back home . . . or something like that." Mama sighed and cupped her wine glass without taking a sip.

She swished the wine around a bit and then closed her eyes as if trying to drown the thought.

"But I was already driving with a heavy heart. I wonder if that's what brought her to me. She senses sadness, some people claim. Anyway, I was driving back from the shop, where Johanna had told me that Five Bop had just told him that this Moipone girl is spreading lies about Basi. I mean, Basi, how well do you even know this girl?"

She looked right at him and I saw sorrow in her eyes.

Basi looked right back at her without flinching and said, "Only a little bit."

I involuntarily cleared my throat. My back felt cold.

"Was she the one at the rugby match?" Papa recalled, narrowing his eyes.

Basi nodded.

"We've only seen her once, then?"

"Yes, Papa."

"So it can't be serious."

Basi clenched his jaw.

"*Hao!* Then why is she saying these things? Rape? *Rape? Whose child* is she?" Mama said spitefully. This time, her words called into question the integrity of a family, and I remembered how, just moments earlier, she had talked about the people who had loved Vera. The difference was not at all subtle.

Basi stood up and started walking out of the room.

"Basimane, come back!" Papa's voice roared. "Tell me something. What do you know about her?"

Basi slid one hand into his pocket, leaned against the door frame and casually scratched his head.

"Ummm . . . not much. She lives with her mother. She's . . . she's a nice girl, I guess."

I almost stood up. I turned abruptly and glared at him, but he didn't look my way.

Instead, he continued casually, "Ja. She's very pretty." He shrugged. "I don't know. I mean . . . I was just getting to know her."

"Sit down," Papa demanded. "This is not to be taken lightly. If this girl is saying these things, we should listen. People can try to ruin what you have, who you are. When they do that, you should pay attention."

Basi came back to sit down.

I wanted to say: *You knew her better than "only a little bit."* But what strange and disconcerting territory I was finding myself in! Questioning my brother? Not supporting him in front of our parents? It seemed absurd. And when all was said and done, it was true that Basi had never really spoken to me about Moipone, wasn't it? I hardly knew how "serious" their relationship was.

Instead, I tried, I really tried. I tried so hard to find alternate ways to view that scene.

And I didn't say anything. It made sense, in those days.

"A woman is questioning your character as a man," said Papa. "She's challenging you and questioning who you are—who everyone," his hand swept across the room, "*everyone*, thinks you are."

We all listened quietly as if he was not only addressing Basi, but all of us, as a family. As if he was saying that the integrity of our family was being questioned. Certainly, Basi alone represented our family. He was the son. The bearer of the torch that was our family name. He alone would carry it into another generation, while I was bound to drop it like a careless child with buttery hands. It had always seemed to me to be an accusation that Basi would *marry* someone while I would *get married*.

My father could speak with such self-assured authority. Finally he leaned forward, pressed his elbows against his thighs, and pointed at Basi.

"Don't walk out of the room. Think about how you're going to handle this. Think about how, as a man, you're going to handle it."

Basi stood still, straightened up and looked my father in the eye. Nodding slowly he said, "I'll handle it."

This speech—along with many other things, of course—would haunt me for years and years to come. I would think back to it and cringe because if there was anything Basi didn't do, it was *handle* the accusations.

"OK. OK!" Mama was suddenly cheered up. "Look. You have a dance coming up. Let's not let this ruin the dance. Are you taking Dineo?"

Of course not, I thought.

"Yes," he said.

I gasped and Mama glared at me. "Who else would he take, Naledi? What other girl would be worthy?"

There wasn't really an answer to that.

So, of course, that Friday in my room I knew what Ole was on about. I suspected she already knew my deepest, darkest secret.

She leaned against the wall beside the window and let her hand hang out, another freshly lit cigarette between her fingers. She stared straight ahead and I was grateful she was not still glaring at me.

I went to put on a CD. Toni Braxton's low voice emerged like a slow, seductive moan, matching the softening light of the late afternoon.

Ole said, "OK. Tell me something else then."

I put on a pair of white shoes with very small heels—the highest Mama would let me wear. I looked at the shoes in the mirror, trying to decide if they went well with a black skirt that I had just pulled on under a blue dress.

Ole took her time.

"Tell me why you think your brother has stopped speaking to Moipone," she eventually said.

"I didn't know—"

"You were in the car on Monday. Tell me why you think he did that. Twice now I've seen him leave her house in a rush."

Now it made sense why Basi had been so late to the shop and why he and Papa had had a fight. He must have had an inkling that Moipone was not going to be quiet about what had happened.

"I don't know."

Ole remained calm and didn't turn to look at me.

"You don't know," she said like she was carefully calculating her next move. Then she took a long puff of her cigarette.

"Nope!" I blurted, a pitiful attempt at sounding nonchalant.

This time she did look at me, even if it was only her head that turned.

Feeling my hands shake, I pressed them to my lower back and continued, "Maybe it's about the dance? I don't know. Maybe they had a fight? Who knows? Who knows what happens between two people. They say: *Taba ke tsa babedi.* We—you and I—can't really know, can we?"

I had put on and taken off three different pairs of shoes by the time I stopped talking. Now I tried to take in deep breaths through my nose. Ole stood in the same position, looking slightly stunned, her mouth open and the cigarette burning away between her fingers. Her eyes went up and down from my face to my now-bare feet as if she were deciding how to meet my challenge. She must have known that I had every intention of acting obtuse.

"Eish!" she exclaimed suddenly, flicking the bud, which had started to burn all the way to her fingers. She sucked them and looked me in the eye. "You know what I think? I think we can know. I think sometimes *taba ke tsa babedi*, that's true, but not always. I think when one of the two people tells you something happened, and you know that that something is wrong, especially . . . " She was moving closer to me. "*Especially* if the person telling you is a girl who says a guy did something awful *to* her, and that that something is *illegal* . . . " She paused, letting me take in the word. "Then I'd have to say that's when *ditaba* stop being *tsa babedi*." She sucked in some air through her teeth and kept her eyes on me.

My heart felt like it would burst through my chest, like I was drowning. I could see the water now, clear above me, blurring the ceiling and softening the light above.

Ole came very close to me, close enough to put both hands on my shoulders. So close that I inhaled her cigarette breath when she spoke.

"Do you know what I'm saying? What I'm talking about?"

I hesitated too long, and time seemed to come to a standstill as the two of us locked eyes, each waiting for the other to speak. Finally I looked down at my bare feet.

Ole made a sharp turn towards the window again, where she stood with her back to me.

"Do you know what a guy once told me?"

I didn't answer.

"One day," she said, "I was just walking to the shop. It was a really nice, warm day and I was excited about going to a Boxing Day picnic. I was going to the shop—your shop—to buy more bread and cooldrinks. Hm!" She shook her head. "So I was just walking along happily, when one of those guys—you know the ones who sit there on the shop stoep all day doing nothing—well, he said something. For everyone to hear. And it was a bit of a surprise because normally those guys don't whistle at me like they do with other girls. And this time there was no one I knew sitting there. So one of them said, 'Eish, this one just needs to be raped. That will fix her.' "

We both took in the silence in the room as Toni finished a song.

"I nearly ran. But I didn't. I told myself: Don't show them you're scared. That's when they'll come after you."

I sank into a chair and looked at Ole's back. Her pants were baggy the way she liked them, her shoes and shirt were men's and so was her hat. It wasn't a stretch at all for me to picture what she was saying. I could see it. I could see the group of boys sitting in the entrance to the shop calling out to girls— every girl who walked by—saying, "Eish, baby, I like your butt," or, "Come to my house and let someone touch those *dikola-molora* for a while." And if they got a glare instead of a smile: "Eish, you're actually really ugly and I was just calling you to make you feel better," or even worse, "Ah, come on. Next week you'll be begging me to touch you! *Sies!*"

So, yes, I could picture Ole walking by and hearing that.

But my brother is not one of those guys.

As I watched her standing there, still as a stick, I realized for a moment, and perhaps for the very first time, how terrifying it must be to be her, walking around Kasi every day. I couldn't imagine being her, with the knowledge of unidentified dead bodies and Vera-the-Ghost and hearing people's contempt for her spoken out loud. And it was really shameful, I suddenly felt, that having been such close friends for most of our lives, I was only now thinking about it.

As if she had just read my thoughts, Ole turned around but her eyes wandered slowly around the room unsure what to fix themselves on. I saw that they were clouded with tears, which I would never see spilling because Ole never let anyone make her cry.

"You live in cars," she said, her voice soft and measured. "You go from your parents' car to your parents' house with its high walls and security gates. You don't know anything." This last bit she said with unveiled resentment.

"But those guys . . . Ole, those guys are horrible. But they're not like my brother." I sounded a bit like my mother, separating us from them.

Seeing Ole's reaction, I immediately regretted not keeping quiet.

"They're *exactly* like him," she hissed. "Didn't he grow up here? Aren't they his friends? Doesn't he say they're his brothers? Doesn't he spend as much time as he can down there? What makes *him* special?"

I sobbed. I threw myself on my bed, right into the heap of clothes. I took a pillow and put it on top of my head and sobbed and sobbed and sobbed.

"You saw them go into the room together, right?" She pulled the pillow off my head.

I sobbed.

"You saw them. You know. You know what you saw."

I don't know how she knew, and I didn't think about what it meant. I was just terrified of what people would think of Basi.

Her voice was merciless above my head. She didn't seem to care, or even notice, that I was crying.

"You don't know the things that have happened to me," she hissed again. "You don't know."

For a while there was nothing but the sound of my sobbing.

Finally, she spoke more calmly. "Sorry," she started. "You know, the best thing is just for someone to say that it's true. When something like this happens, the girl just wants someone to say it's true. To believe her. Nedi . . . ," she started in her best conspiratorial tone. "If you tell me that it's true and I tell Moipone that you said so, I think . . . I just think that she would feel better. I think just knowing that someone believes her would really, really help."

I stopped crying and sat up. Ole walked around my bed and took a tissue from my red tissue box. Slowly she walked back and sat at the edge of the bed, handing me the tissue. When she looked at me I noticed that her eyes had softened.

"I could tell her that you said it was true. Only her mother believes her now. No one else. Do you know that Aus' Nono said she was lying? So many people . . . so many people have told her that Basi would never hurt anyone." Ole paused, then added, "I saw Moipone's mother cry."

I felt overwhelming pity.

"No one believes her. Remember Aus' Joyce from our street? When Moipone walked past her house yesterday, Aus' Joyce yelled, 'You should feel lucky! Raped by Basimane? You should have said thank you.' "

I thought of Moipone walking to school, her heart heavy, her thoughts scattered with the fear of what might happen next— and then hearing that.

"It's funny—all these people always loved Moipone. But no one gets more love than Basi, *nè*? I mean, you know that. You live with him. You know that."

I felt an unbearable mix of fury towards Ole, and anger fused with love and a sense of duty towards my brother.

"Everyone makes mistakes—" I started.

Ole sat still, nodded like she was interested in every word that I had to say.

I continued, between sobs, "It was only one time. Probably a misunderstanding. I'm sure . . . I'm sure he's very sorry because . . . That's not who he is, the type of person who would do that. I'm sure it's not what he meant . . . A mistake . . . " I felt more and more hopeless as my voice trailed off.

Ole nodded and I felt we were in agreement, at least, about it being *unlike* Basi. That it was *out of character*.

"That will make her feel so much better," was the last thing Ole said that day.

21

ON THE EVENING OF THE DANCE, the last evening that my brother would be home, I remember him coming to my room and standing at my door.

"You look stunning, Nedi."

I had decided on the black skirt and the white flowy top. Kitsano had phoned me a few minutes earlier and said, "I have a red rose and a white rose but I didn't know which one you'd like better."

I had started to regain my excitement about the dance, thinking things were about to take a turn for the better.

"Thanks," I told Basi, who looked handsome in his black pants, an unbuttoned white shirt and a pair of brand-new shiny black shoes. He leaned casually against the door frame and crossed his feet, ever suave and self-assured, like a movie star in a leading role.

"Are you OK?" I asked him, putting on my lipstick in front of the mirror.

"Of course," he said. "It's going to be great. We can just forget everything and enjoy the night."

Without looking at him I brushed on some blush and tried to sound casual when I said, "You're happy to be going with Dineo?"

Too quickly, Basi said, "Yep. She's fun." He looked at his watch. "Oops! We should start moving."

Everything's going to be fine, I kept saying to myself, despite the dread I felt in the pit of my stomach.

My brother held out his elbow for me and I tucked in my hand as we walked to meet our parents in the kitchen.

Mama was taking yet another "last" picture of us when Five Bop rang our intercom. In a moment he was in our kitchen, breathlessly explaining that Moipone and her mother had gone to the police only a few minutes before. When he was finished talking he sat himself on the wooden kitchen chairs our mother had gone to Cape Town to buy. For a moment it occurred to me that I had never seen Five sitting in our house before—but there he was, taking a sip of water from one of our expensive imported glasses.

But Basi, Mama, and Papa were suddenly rushing around between Basi's room and the car.

"You can buy more when you get there!" Mama was yelling.

In the midst of the chaos, Five's comment sounded rather casual to my ears.

"Ole claims you told her it was true. Can you believe that?" His contempt for Ole was barely veiled.

There was a pause before, one by one, the members of my family turned to look at me. I heard nothing but water bubbles.

When I finally managed to speak, I said, "I just said I saw Moipone . . . that she was here and she was . . . she was . . . uh . . . "

"She was what, Naledi?!" My mother slapped her thigh impatiently.

"She was . . . Her blouse was torn."

They all stared at me for what felt like an interminable amount of time.

Then Papa yelled, "We don't have time to waste!" and they all scrambled around me. I reached for the chair, feeling that I may be about to fall to the spinning floor.

In a minute they were in the car and Five and I were standing outside watching with stunned expressions as the three of them rolled over the pebbles towards the gates, which were slowly opening.

About a metre away from us, the car came to a standstill.

Mama rolled down the window and glared at me.

"You shame us."

To my absolute shock, Basi then rolled down the window and yelled, "I'll phone you, OK? It's OK, Nedi!"

On the street the sound of the car quickly faded away.

Five shook his head. "You didn't say anything, *akere?*"

I hung my head and cried.

Five said, "*Tsk, tsk.* Naledi, it's a rough world for a Black man. He only has family to count on."

I felt pathetic, wiping my face and looking at Five, hoping he'd say something comforting.

Then he said, "Basi would never—"

I shook my head vigorously and cut him off.

"I know. He wouldn't."

That was the last time I would see my brother for a very long time.

22

"DO YOU REMEMBER, a long time ago, there was a body found in the woods?" Aus' Johanna roused me out of my daydreaming. I had been sitting on a high chair at the counter on a very slow afternoon, waiting for customers.

The mood around our house had made the shop the best place to be and since my brother had gone, I was at the shop every chance I could get.

Aus' Johanna was dusting and repositioning stock on the shelves, and I had been eyeing a magazine without picking it up. I was constantly finding myself drifting away with my thoughts, unable to remember what I had just heard or what I was supposed to be doing at school and at home. So when Aus' Johanna spoke, I nearly jumped off the chair.

"Yes!" I almost yelled. "Yes, I remember the body. I still think about it." I was nodding away, rubbing my eyes, my head racing back to all the bits and pieces I remembered about the body.

"So you know, the other day, I'm telling my brother about how I used to have this skirt. This really beautiful little skirt that I miss and how I liked wearing it with these shoes." Aus' Johanna liked to start right at the beginning and tell elaborate stories.

I sat back and settled in to hear it.

"So." She smoothed the back of her skirt, all ladylike, and sat down in the chair facing me. She licked her lips and shook her head before she continued, and I wondered how her lipstick stayed so perfect for such a long time. "*Heh!* So he says, '*Heh wena*, Jo, I remember that dress. Didn't you wear it for Kemang's twenty-first?'"

Aus' Johanna looked at me as if I was supposed to understand the significance of this but I only stared back curiously. She had lines crinkling her forehead but she smoothed them with both hands, delicately caressing the creases with her fingertips. She opened her eyes wide as if she were waking herself from a deep sleep or a wandering thought.

"So. I remember that party. Do you remember that party?" Aus' Johanna sometimes told me about people and places and expected me to know exactly what she was talking about. When I inevitably didn't—since she was a good ten years older than me and didn't have any of the same friends—she still looked puzzled.

"I don't remember," I said and shook my head, suggesting that I had merely forgotten.

"That was a good party. It was nice. A lot of people I know were having their twenty-firsts that year and I wore that skirt and those shoes to many parties." She laughed at the memory and clapped her hands. "*Iyooo!* And I was still with Makhaola," she added.

Makhaola had been her first and only boyfriend for many years and I always got the sense that she still loved and missed him.

"That's when you heard about the body," I tried to bring her back.

"*Hoh!* That body. *Ah, ah, aaahh!* That body . . . that was a girl who had been at that party."

I inhaled sharply. After all these years?

"That's what my brother tells me. He says, 'Eish, Jo. That was a wild party. You know those guys from Jozi? They had come with that girl from there. She was a good friend of one of the guys.' And, and . . . and so she had come along with him and his friends. She didn't know anyone here."

A customer stood at the counter in front of us and said, "One packet chips." I jumped, so engrossed was I in the story.

Aus' Johanna stood up and walked over to the customer, her shoes clap-clapping against her heels. Aus' Johanna always walked around the shop like she was at a time-sensitive business event. She dressed like it too. I watched impatiently as she picked up the money, reached over to the chips shelf and turned to the till to get the customer's change.

Someone walked in through the door and I was relieved when they went over to the fridge to select some meat instead of coming to the counter. It felt like it had been a year before Aus' Johanna came back over to sit next to me.

"What happened to her?" I said quickly.

"She was—" She turned her head to the door, waved at someone and said, "*O kae?*" before turning back to me.

She smoothed her skirt again. Aus' Johanna was always in the process of grooming.

"I was still telling you about the girl."

"Yes! The body—the girl!"

"Hey, she's not just a body, *wena!* She was a woman, just like you and me. And then she was killed!" As she said "killed" she gave a loud *clap!* with her hands.

"They know who killed her?"

"Raped and killed. One of the men who had come with her finally confessed. He told the police he hadn't slept in years. Said he wanted to die because, *heheeee*—" She pressed her fingers to her eyes and shook her head. "Because he said that girl comes to him at night. Tortures him . . . *heh!*"

"Nightmares?"

"Stop chewing your nails. Did you just start doing that? A girl needs to look beautiful. No boy wants to see chewed-up nails."

"Sorry."

"Paint them nicely and then you'll get a boyfriend."

"OK."

"Eish, what was I saying? *Hoh* . . . the boy. No, nightmares? No, not nightmares. Nightmares are dreams. *A se toro!* He sees her. She comes. She comes like Vera-the-Ghost . . .

"Naledi? What's wrong? *Ha haaa!* Don't be scared. She won't come to you! Now you're scared. Did I scare you? Don't worry, man. It's his problem . . .

"Naledi? *Ke eng?* Are you afraid of ghosts?

"Naledi? Don't cry. *Hao!* Why are you crying? Shame, it breaks your heart, doesn't it? I know. It broke my heart too. I wanted to cry when my brother told me . . .

"*Heh!* That's being a woman in the world. These are the things men do . . . You have to be careful. You have to protect yourself."

"But I suppose she thought she was protected because he was her best friend, huh?" I eventually managed.

"Eish . . . ah! You never know."

"*Re tla re eng?*"

"Imagine. Someone she knew so well . . . " After a long pause in which her thoughts seemed to take her far away, she said, "My mother said there is a reason why most ghosts are women. Here, use my tissue . . .

"You can't say anything? Don't speak. *O sa wara. O sa lela,* Nedi. That's how things happen between men and women sometimes. Watch who you call your friends. Men have different needs . . . It's natural. All men have those needs. Watch who you call your friends," she kept saying. "Be careful of the drunks and the cowards."

"You said this guy was her friend," I reminded her, between sobs.

"Ja," she said. "But maybe he never really was. Maybe he

always looked at her a certain way. You see?"

And how did you know? I thought. *How does any girl know?*
Aus' Johanna's eyes suddenly got wider. "It's the thing
Moipone doesn't realize."

I sat up. "What?"

"That men have needs. That you can't just go to a guy's
house alone with him and go to his bedroom and—"

"His bedroom?"

"Yes, I heard she went into his bedroom and—"

"Who told you that?"

"Joyce, who lives next door to me. I don't know how she
could have gone there in a short skirt and a sexy top and lain
on his bed and expected us to believe she didn't know what
was going to happen."

She waved to someone else and asked after his children
before continuing.

"And she was his girlfriend, not just some friend. She was his
girlfriend and she went into his bedroom. How can a man rape
his girlfriend? It's like saying a man raped his wife. It's stupid.
It's nonsense."

"I don't know . . . I don't think she went into his room. I
think we don't know the whole truth—"

Aus' Johanna slapped me lightly on my wrist. "*Heh!* Nedi,
this is your brother, *wena*. I heard you said something to Ole. I
hope it's not true." She gave me a warning look. "Your brother
would never do that to you, would he? Stop saying there's this
story and that story. Everyone knows what Ole wanted, so let's
not talk about Ole. We all saw the way she looked at Moipone."
She clicked her tongue. "*Sies!* She's not even ashamed! *Mxm.*"
She smoothed her skirt again. "But you are a different story.
Support your brother. Stop saying we don't know the truth.
Basi knows the truth."

"Basi and Moipone?"

"Yes, the two of them. But she's not telling the truth."

I nodded, just to calm her wrath.

"Nedi, did you know—*did you know*—that she was at Nkele's doing her hair the morning before the party? What was she expecting? Nkele says she asked her to make it look beautiful. *Heh?* Who knows why she's lying? Maybe she wanted fame. Maybe she slept with someone else and she wants her mother to think she was raped. Some women check their girls, you know. Maybe her mother knows she's not a virgin any more and this is how she's explaining herself."

A few weeks later a story circulated in Kasi about how Moipone had slept with a guy from school and hadn't come home the night before, and when her mother asked her if she was still a virgin, she said Basi had raped her.

The story stuck for a long time. I'd say that if you went to Marapong today and asked those who are still around, those who tell the tale like an old location classic, that is the version you'd get.

EPILOGUE

YOU DO KNOW MY BROTHER, don't you? I've been thinking it's best I don't continue without acknowledging that probability. It would be insulting, I think.

Of course you know him; he lives right here, and if you haven't seen him you've probably, definitely, heard of him. You admire him, I expect. Maybe you watched him defend those men last year, or you were among the many who followed that very famous case of those women a few years ago. Yes, the whole country knows him. What impresses you more, I wonder? That he is so young, so arrestingly handsome? Or is it his ever-determined and, as some have put it, "fierce and unprecedented" pursuit of justice?

For me, it is all of these things.

Through the years I've bumped into many old girls from school, now grown women, some with families and some without, all of them with fond memories—and enduring admiration—for my brother. All of them excitedly remind me that they "knew Basi when . . . "

"Why did he ever leave?" some will ask.

"I can't believe how that all happened," others are still saying.

"I'm still shocked at what some women will do to one of our own men," a few have told me angrily.

One person I've seen more times than I care to is Dineo. She works as a doctor in Tshwane, along with many of the people we went to school with. I see her because we move in some of the same circles, meaning that we're still friends with some old girls and because our mothers' friendship has stood the test of time.

"Dineo still loves Basi," Mama has told me too many times. "She still phones him."

I'm sure.

But Basi has never mentioned her. Not since he left. I know from Dineo that they sometimes did see each other when they were both at varsity. Dineo says they "have drinks or whatever," once in a while.

Basi doesn't speak of the past as much as the rest of us do.

In fact, the only time I spoke to him about the old days, the first time, was just a few months ago, when I said to him, "Ole teaches at Wits." I think there has always been this urge to say something, but I never could. For years I haven't even been able to mention people from home, people we grew up with—old friends about whom we should normally be able to chat and laugh. I don't even wonder out loud about someone like Five Bop. But that day I felt bold, for some reason. Maybe because it was the day following a particularly difficult night.

I had been in the bath for the better part of it, turning the tap on and off until there was no hot water left. It was in the days following my accidental meeting with Moipone.

So after I told him about Ole, Basi shook his head and laughed.

"*Tjo!* Nedi, you're still friends with Ole?"

As if she were an amusing, distant memory.

"Basi, you're still friends with Kgosi," I said.

We were at Basi's house in one of the new suburbs around Menlyn. He had been busy cleaning his very flashy black BMW—something he says he does to "clear his head." My brother has so many cases these days that his work leaves him with very little time to himself. When he is home, he savours his quality time. Some days he drives to Kgosi's house just across the street, and the two of them wash their cars together. Kgosi, now an engineer, has the same car in red.

Basi leaned out from the passenger seat where he had been wiping the red-leather seats and said, "Come on. It's not the same."

"Why not? We're all childhood friends," I countered.

Basi looked down at the ground and clenched his jaw.

"Why not?" I persisted, feeling bolder than I had in years, my ears burning hotter than they had since the day Basi had left and Mama had said, "You shame us."

Basi's head ducked in and he busied his hands with wiping the dashboard. I stood in front of the car, its black metal glistening in the sun, its two doors wide open and its powerful speakers blaring an old Babyface song, and I waited for my brother to say something.

For the first time I was ready to speak to him. Answer his questions, if he had any, admit what I had done, defend myself if I had to.

I listened to the sound of my head throbbing and my heart pounding and refused to let my hands fidget. I willed my feet to stay put. I waited and waited as the white cloth moved back and forth over the dashboard and my brother said nothing.

Finally his head came out of the car. Instead of looking at me, he picked up the bucket of dirty, soapy water and walked over to the outdoor basin. He took his time. Finally, he turned and walked towards me.

At the car Basi leaned his back against the bonnet and put his hands delicately but firmly in front of him.

I lost my nerve a bit then, found myself thinking that maybe I would just let it go, maybe it wasn't worth it. What did I have to gain, I wondered, now that it was all done and in the past? It was such a long time ago . . .

When Basi's eyes finally rose from the ground, they landed

firmly and unwaveringly on mine. I forced myself to stare back. I have a difficult time looking people in the eye. My eyes tend to move around. I've never been as calm and comfortable with myself as my brother is. But meeting his gaze seemed to rattle him a little bit. I found myself facing a slightly uncomfortable and surprised-looking Basi.

In a second, though, Basi gathered himself. I was reminded of that day, a long time ago, when I had seen him so nervous as he got ready to see Moipone, and then how quickly he had stilled and composed himself.

I'm no match for my brother, I thought hopelessly.

Basi forced a soft, pitying smile.

"Listen. That girl hurt our family," he finally said. "You know that."

His eye twitched and then he blurted, "Ole hurt our family! Running to the police, taking something you had told her out of context—"

"What?!" I surprised myself by throwing my arms in the air, but then watched, mortified, as spittle flew from my mouth and landed on the just-cleaned car.

Basi followed its move as it started trickling like a single tear down the black of the car.

He didn't move or say anything as I turned sharply and marched to the basin, retrieved the dry white cloth that he had been using. He stood staring at me with no expression as I reached over and rubbed the spit longer and harder than I needed to. Like I was having a tantrum at age five.

Shame on you, I reprimanded myself. *Even today? Even now, after everything, you still can't say anything to him?*

"Nedi, look . . . I'm not angry with you."

It was like calling your parents' house and hearing a stranger's voice answer the phone.

"Angry?" I heard my voice say.

"Yes," he said without moving, his eyes squarely on mine. "I know it was never your fault. I know . . . " he said and started moving towards me. "I know what kind of person—what kind of *sister*—you are."

I was confused, my heart softening, my body relaxing as he put his hands firmly on my shoulders. There was something in my throat, my eyes spilling over.

My brother held me and said, "You wouldn't have done that. You wouldn't have done something so despicable. Something that was such a lie. *Such* a lie." His arms held me tightly, as if protecting me from my own misunderstanding.

What could I do or say? Here was my opportunity to say no, that I had understood very well what had happened, that he had committed a crime. But hadn't I always wanted him to tell me that I was wrong? Hadn't I always wanted him to tell me that my limited understanding of sex had confused me? What would you have said?

I said nothing.

Basi started walking away from me, bucket in his hand.

I don't know what it was. Maybe the rage I felt when he turned around and winked. Maybe the easy, carefree way he swung the bucket. Maybe it was the relaxed Basi swagger. Or maybe—and I suspect this is it—maybe it was the crunch-crunch-crunch of his feet in his own pebbled walkway. I'll never understand how that sound doesn't squeeze at his heart.

I tried to control my voice, but it came out sounding as enraged as I felt.

"It happened to me too, you know," I started my lie.

Basi swung around, sending water flying.

"What?" he said, his face contorted with confusion.

"A guy did that to me. It was at varsity . . . " I was shaking from fury and my lie. I put both hands on my cheeks and willed myself to stand still, my eyes focussing on the stones on the ground. "This guy . . . We were going out and he—well, we went to his room all the time, but this time, I guess . . . I don't know . . . "

I went to sit down on a chair near the car, kept my hands on my cheeks and my eyes on the ground.

Basi rushed to me and crouched in front of me.

I took a deep breath. "Anyway . . . long story short—"

"No! No long story short! I can't believe this happened to you! What? When? Why didn't you tell? Nedi, don't cut the story short. They force women to tell the whole story in court. You'd better tell me . . . I'm your brother."

"Basi, stop. He was my boyfriend and he was sure I had misunderstood. That I had wanted the same thing."

My brother raised my chin so that we were locking eyes.

"Nedi," he said, and I could feel the rage in his voice. I could imagine it rising from the pit of his stomach, and I could see him fighting to stay calm. After a breath or two, his well-practised lawyer voice was so calm that what he said next sounded perfectly reasonable. "I'll kill him! Who was it? I'll find out and—"

"Basi . . . " I tried to sound like an understanding counsellor. Once, at varsity, I had gone to see a counsellor, but only once. She had spoken to me like she was a mother and I a child, and I'd resented her for her forced, unfamiliar sweetness. I never went back, but now I tried her voice on Basi. "I think that's what Moipone thought. I think she was, maybe, I don't know, but I think she thought it was . . . forced."

Basi stood up abruptly. "It's not the same thing!"

"Maybe . . . But it could be, couldn't it?"

"Nedi, it was so long ago! I was young . . . You don't understand."

"Tell me what I don't understand."

Basi stared at the ground for a very long time. When he

finally looked up he said, "It just . . . It got out of hand. It wasn't . . . " He bit his lip and blinked a few times. "You're not taught to read women's minds. You're taught that they want whatever you want."

Would you call that an admission of guilt?

We were both still for a while. We listened to the breeze brushing against the leaves and the faint sound of music coming from inside the car.

"Basi—" I started after a while.

"It was a long time ago," he said sternly. With finality. "I would never, *never* . . . even as a young man . . . She was my girlfriend and . . . She knew . . . she exp—" He pressed his palm against his forehead and wiped off the beads of sweat that had accumulated around his hairline.

"Basi—"

"Enough, Naledi." He shut his eyes as if willing away a thought, or a memory. "I don't want to bring it up again." He slowly walked away from me.

I wanted to say: *It doesn't feel like a long time ago to her, or to me.*

But he was gone. And so was another piece of what my brother and I used to have.

It was only hours after that, when I emerged cold and wrinkled from another bath, that I started to feel something close to pity for my brother. I remembered the way he had looked at the ground, the way he had said, "It was a long time ago." The look of wanting to extinguish a burning memory.

I thought: *That's the difference between Basi and anyone else. He knows. He knows it was wrong and I am willing to say that when he's alone, he calls it what it is, gives it its proper name. "Rape," not "a misunderstanding." Maybe after a glass of wine or a good laugh with Kgosi the thought creeps away, but he knows. He knows the difference.*

A few days after Basi had left in such a hurry that night long ago, Mama sat me down and told me exactly what was going to happen: Basi was going to finish high school at a private boys' school in Cape Town, an even more prestigious and exclusive one than his old school. He was going to be away from home for the remainder of the year, and when we wanted to see him, we would go to him.

"It's very expensive, but he's had a tough time and deserves it," she told me, her sideways glare spelling out my betrayal.

We didn't talk about what I had said or who I had said it to. We just went on pretending that nothing had happened. My parents took me to school every day the way they had always done, and I went to the shop and did my job. I studied very hard as it was the one obvious thing I could do to apologize to my family, and by the end of matric my marks were impressive.

My parents "made it all go away," as they put it.

"No one will be asking questions or looking for Basi," Papa told me. "And I don't want us, as a family, making life any harder than it already is."

Basi lived well in Cape Town, seemed to forget everything except his friends, especially Kgosi. Kgosi went to join him at varsity, where they shared a room and then a flat. Now they live across the street from each other and are in love with professional women who went to the same kinds of schools that Basi and I went to, just in different cities.

He's fine, my brother. He's doing better than anyone else I know.

I don't know much about Moipone because I hardly ever saw her again. She stopped coming to the shop; she changed to a high school a lot farther away.

I stopped speaking to Ole after Basi left. She was right in

saying that Moipone needed someone to believe her. My words were as close as she could get to an admission by my brother, so she took that to the police. That didn't do anything for her in the end though.

In the days following my brother's departure there was just one conversation with Ole—no, it was a confrontation—in which she raged on about the injustice of it.

"Him with his lion shirt and his Nike tekkies! I knew he was up to something that day! I knew he didn't want me to come up to *di*Ex with you . . . I knew . . . "

I walked away from her when her rising voice started attracting attention in the middle of the street.

It didn't matter, though. It didn't make people think less of Basi. Most of the girls just wanted to know why he had transferred to Cape Town.

"It's a better school for getting into varsity," was our family's rehearsed answer and the one I gave everyone, including my friends Limakatso and Kelelo.

I missed my brother sorely. I would go into his room and just sit on his bed, looking around at his things, now neatly arranged around the bed and on the dressing table. His clothes had been scattered on the bed and the floor until Mama had made a trip down to Cape Town—her second in the first month.

And in those first few weeks after he left I was more heart-broken about not seeing my brother than I was about what had happened to Moipone. I felt paralyzing guilt, especially when my parents looked at me a certain way, or those days when Mama would openly weep for her son, who had "unneces-sarily missed his formal" and who "never did anything wrong." I hated Ole and didn't want to have anything to do with her; I didn't speak to her for the remainder of our time in high school, which was four years. I wasn't sorry that we went to different universities—she stayed near home while I went to

Durban, halfway between my parents and my brother. I didn't see Ole when I came home for the holidays, although I did see Basi. We didn't ever mention why he had left.

Ole was out of my life until about a year ago when I saw her at a cafeteria at Wits, where I'm now studying African literature and she's lecturing in Political Science. We greeted each other very politely and carried on as if we were new friends getting to know each other—cautious, but willing.

It's true that I'd like to know more about how Moipone is, but I can't ask anyone. No one really knows much about her.

The only time that Ole and I ever mentioned the past was when she said, "Whatever happened to Kitsano?"

I don't know. I had stood him up and was too young and too inept at handling relationships to phone him. I heard he had waited for me at the formal and that he was upset to hear our family had had a "sudden crisis," as I told my friends. The fact is that my interest in boys and relationships had gone from exciting to . . . well, confusing, at best.

For years before going to varsity I avoided boys. I started wearing jeans and put away the short skirts and the sexy blouses. I started thinking really seriously about never kissing another boy, just in case we had a . . . "misunderstanding." You know, just in case we were not on the same page about things. Because I reckoned if something did happen, I may not be in a good position to warrant support.

Being a girl.

And being the girl who betrayed her brother.

When I saw Moipone that day, when she looked up and saw me staring at her scar, she said, "I wish him a lot of bad luck." She said it very calmly, very matter-of-factly, and then she walked away.

The difference between my brother and me is that being special helps you pick and choose between what matters and what doesn't and, sometimes, what's real and what isn't. I think he has chosen to tuck away that chapter of his life in some safe, dark place and has refused to visit it.

For Moipone, I think, there's never been that choice.

For me there's never been that choice.

What would it be like to be that adored and that revered? To have people say you're next to holy, so you can decide for yourself if you're angry or not? Guilty or not?

I've always sensed a connection to Moipone, a feeling that we belong in the same corner of the room, or something like that. Perhaps it comes from being aware of the loss of dignity and sense of safety that she endured. I remember always the feeling of being afraid of my brother after I had witnessed the rape, the confusion and utter devastation I felt when I thought of him. I've understood that she must have felt all that and worse. And when he managed to fly away from it, come away unscathed, everyone said she was a tainted liar.

"Who is she to be raped by Basi?" someone had said. Feeling, I think, that it would be an honour, not an absolute violation. "Why would someone like him need to find someone like her for sex? He could have had anyone." Seeing Moipone—and not the rape—as being beneath Basi.

My mother and aunts tell me that my loyalty should only be to family. Yet their loyalty is only to my brother. No one imagines that I was scarred by what I knew. Never mind that Moipone's life was devastated by what happened to her.

"She's not your mother's child, that girl," they've told me when I've dared to bring up the possibility that Moipone may not have been lying. "Protect your own," they insist.

I know that Basi and I share something Moipone will never understand, but all these years I've known that Moipone and I share something that Basi will never understand. There are different types of family in the world. Are we sisters? I think so.

We move like impalas among hunting lions. Moipone knows it, so does Ole, and so do I.

Basi is a man, and that's good enough, but he's also more than that. He's the boy—the much-loved and adored boy—with luck and looks and brains. He manages to fend off misfortune (and his own struggles are, of course, not minor) with the ease of wiping dust off a shiny shoe. In many ways, as much as possible, he will always be cocooned in the loyalty of his parents, his friends, and the women who love him, whatever he does. I know they can't protect him from a lot of what he experiences in his world. I know that. I understand that he's not living in a world he can trust either. But I also know that my mother and his friends see him as infinitely faultless. Who hasn't heard of my brother or someone like him?

After my parents had swiftly sent him away, Mama told me, "He's going to be what the gods intended him to be. He can go anywhere he wants to go, be whoever he wants to be." Her arm swept across the room, her bangles chiming softly. "Anything he wants."

Her eyes looked at me steadily as she declared with unwavering confidence, "He can be the *president*, if he wants to be."

You know she's right.

GLOSSARY

akere (Setswana) isn't it true
A se toro! (Setswana) It's not a dream.
aus' (Setswana) short for "ausi," sister
Aus' o pila, waitse? (Setswana) Sister, you are beautiful, you know?
ayeye (Setswana) you're in trouble
bathong (Setswana) people (an exclamation of exasperation)
bogobe (Setswana) porridge
bop (slang) refers to cents, counted in tens (5 bop is 50 cents)
cherrie (slang) girlfriend
deurmekaar (Afrikaans) confused
Di a bowa! (Setswana) It's busy!
diketo (Setswana) game of throwing stones
dikolamolora (Setswana) the first showing of breasts at puberty
ditori (Setswana) stories, often used to mean "lies"
dula (Setswana) sit
ee (Setswana) yes
Eeeh! Bana! (Setswana) Hey! Kids!
eeng (Setswana) yes
e fedile (Setswana) it is finished
etla (Setswana) come
'fana (isiZulu) short for "umfana," young boy
haai (Setswana) no
Hao! (Setswana) Oh!
haua (Setswana) no
hee-lee-lee (Setswana) the sound of ululating
heh (Setswana) hey
Iyo! Tshabang! Shianang! (Setswana) Hey! Run away! Run!
jo (slang) my friend
ka nnete (Setswana) it's true
Ke eng? (Setswana) What is it?
kepisi (Setswana) cap
Khante? (Setswana) And so?
khati (Setswana) skipping rope, where two people hold the ends
ko (Setswana) in
ko motseng (Setswana) in the village
ko Tshwene (Setswana) Tshwene's shop
Lege ba re eng. (Setswana) No matter what they say.

legusha (Setswana) an outdoor jumping game
lekeisheneng (Setswana) location/township
letagwa (Setswana) drunkard
Makhoa (Setswana) Whites
mara (Setswana) but
MK (isiXhosa/isiZulu) short for Umkhonto we Sizwe ("Spear of the Nation")
Mma ngwana o tshwara thipa mo bogaleng. (Setswana) A mother holds
the sharp end of the knife.
mo khoneng (Setswana) on the corner
mo phasiching (Setswana) on the passage
motse (Setswana) village
mxm (Setswana) clicking of the tongue, used disapprovingly
nama (Setswana) meat
nè (Afrikaans) not so?
ngwanake (Setswana) my child
ngwanyana (Setswana) girl
O itshware pila. (Setswana) Behave yourself.
O kae? (Setswana) How are you?
O sa wara. O sa lela. (Setswana) Don't worry. Don't cry.
O tlha kae? (Setswana) Where have you come from?
O tsamae pila. (Setswana) Go well.
ou (Afrikaans) old
Re tla re eng? (Setswana) What can we say?
scafteen (slang) lunch box
sephatlho/diphatlho (Setswana) quarter loaf/loaves of bread with stuffing
inside (bunny chow)
seshabo (Setswana) vegetables
setswadi (Setswana) parent
shoppong (Setswana) the shop
Sies! (Afrikaans) Sis!
Taba ke tsa babedi. (Setswana) News/an affair is between two people.
Tjerr! (Setswana) an expression of irritation
Tjo! (Setswana) Wow!
tshwene (Setswana) monkey
tu (Setswana) please
umfazi (isiZulu) woman
waitse (Setswana) you know
wena (Setswana) (and) you

ACKNOWLEDGEMENTS

I wouldn't have had the courage to write this book without the bravery and inspiration of some of the most dedicated and committed women I know in South Africa: I thank Pumla Dineo Gqola and Gail Smith, for important conversations that offered a lot of insight. Thank you to the many nurses, mothers and other women who work against violence against women, and who took the time to speak to me a few years ago. Thank you to Bra Zakes, who has been very patient and generous and always takes time to answer a frantic email. I'm also grateful to my dear friends Anyes Babillon and Martin Reesink for being kind and generous enough to read and offer very helpful suggestions. Thank you also to Charlotte and Max for continuing to listen to my endless chatter about my work, and for the title suggestions.

I'm also very grateful for the love and support of my dear beloved friend Jude Dibia, and my beloved Rima Vesely-Flad, whose love spans many years and is always close.

Finally I'm most thankful for the ever-present love of my children, Motsumi and Siamela, who give me a new story to tell every day.

KAGISO LESEGO MOLOPE was born and educated in South Africa. Her first novel, *Dancing in the Dust* (Mawenzi House) was on the IBBY Honour List for 2006. Her second novel, *The Mending Season*, was chosen to be on the school curriculum in South Africa. *This Book Betrays My Brother* was awarded the Percy Fitzpatrick Prize by the English Academy of Southern Africa, where it was first published. She lives in Ottawa.